The
TRIMONI
TWINS
and the
SHRUNKEN
TREASURE

Also by Pam Smallcomb

THE LAST BURP
OF MAC McGERP

THE TRIMONI TWINS AND
THE CHANGING COIN

The TRIMONI TWINS

and the SHRUNKEN TREASURE

Pam Smallcomb

BLOOMSBURY
CHILDREN'S
BOOKS

First published in Great Britain in 2006 by Bloomsbury Publishing Plc
36 Soho Square, London, W1D 3QY

First published in the USA in 2005 by Bloomsbury Publishing,
Children's Books, USA
175 Fifth Avenue, New York, NY 10010

A CIP catalogue record of this book is available from the British Library

ISBN 0 7475 7640 8

All papers used by Bloomsbury Publishing are natural, recyclable products
made from wood grown in well-managed forests. The manufacturing
processes conform to the environmental regulations of the country of origin.

Typeset by Hewer Text UK Ltd, Edinburgh
Printed in Great Britain by Clays Ltd, St Ives Plc

1 3 5 7 9 10 8 6 4 2

www.bloomsbury.com

To my husband, Rick, and my editor, Julie Romeis,
with heartfelt thanks for zuufting all my
big problems into little ones.

And to Alex, Caity, Patrick and Lucas for
ka-poofing into quiet little mice so I could write.

CHaPTER ONE

Beezel ran as fast as she could, knowing that if she slowed even for an instant, the big cat would hook her with one of its claws and bring her down.

She tore along the upstairs hallway, her eyes darting back and forth, searching for some place to hide from the enormous creature that was hunting her.

At the end of the hall was an ornate wooden door. Try as she might, Beezel couldn't turn the doorknob. She slammed her body against the door. *Come on! Open! Open!*

Beezel heard a deep throaty growl behind her. She slowly turned and faced her pursuer. As she stared up into the eyes of the giant cat, Beezel's heart beat wildly in her chest. The cat's mouth quivered slightly. The animal wore a thick leather collar around its neck. Attached to the collar was a silver bell. Beezel heard the bell jingle as the cat inched towards her.

Great blathering Blackstone! she thought as she glanced left and right. *I'm trapped!*

She shut her eyes and winced. *That cat's going to kill me!* Beezel opened one eye to watch in spite of herself. She heard a noise above her and looked up at the beamed ceiling. As she did so, a pair of gigantic hands pulled up the roof of the house, just as if it were the lid on a child's toy box.

Beezel felt the air move across her face as the cat began its pounce. Ka-poof. Right before her eyes, the giant cat changed into a snail. Even though it had a new physical form, the cat-turned-snail kept moving slowly towards Beezel, leaving a shiny trail behind it on the floor.

An enormous hand reached down and grabbed Beezel, raising her high up into the air. From its tight grip, Beezel could see the rooftops of the houses around her.

She twisted her head to see the owner of the giant hand. A huge face, with short black hair and piercing blue eyes, stuck itself inches from her own furry brown mouse face. Beezel's whiskers twitched nervously. "Squeak!"

"Beezel, *honestly*," her sister, Mimi, said crossly. "You *do* realise you could have been eaten." She grasped Beezel by her tail and set her down in the centre of the shop floor. Mimi pointed her finger at Beezel. Ka-poof. Beezel changed from a mouse back into herself: the eleven-year-old identical twin of her sister, Mimi.

"Holy Houdini's handkerchief!" Beezel exclaimed. "What took you so long?"

CHAPTER TWO

Beezel stood next to Mimi in the shop and tried to recover from her near-death experience. The cat had almost caught her in the doll's house! She wondered, not for the first time, if ka-poofing would be the end of her someday.

The day had started quite normally, Beezel thought, looking back on it. Their flight from Baltimore to Amsterdam had been completely uneventful.

"This doesn't look like Holland to me," Mimi had said when she stepped off the plane. "It doesn't look different at all."

"It's an *airport*, Mimi," Beezel said. "I think they're pretty much the same everywhere."

Beezel, Mimi and Hector, the twins' tutor, found a taxi and headed for Amsterdam.

As they got closer to the centre of the city, the differences began to appear. Beezel pointed to the rooftops. "Oh, Mimi, look!"

The unusual types of gables on the houses made a wonderful skyline. Some had stepped edges; others were bell shaped with carved ornaments that looked like wedding cakes.

When they came to a stop, Beezel rolled down the taxi window, and the cold air of a crisp spring day blew across her face. The tangy smell of the canal water, mixed with the rich aroma of coffee and baked goods from an outdoor café across the street, wafted into their car.

They drove down roads lined with narrow row houses on one side and canals on the other. The streets, crowded with people riding bikes, rang with the sounds of car horns and bike bells. That's when it hit Beezel: she really was in a foreign country, far away from her home with the Trimoni Circus.

"We're finally here!" Mimi said. "I can't wait to see the Van Gogh Museum!"

"Not today, duck," Hector said. "I've asked the driver to drop us off at my uncle's house. I want to check in on him. He was so strange on the phone when I talked to him last. After we say hello and see that all is well, we'll grab another cab to the hotel."

Hector's favourite uncle, Mathias Hoogaboom, had called a few weeks earlier and insisted that his nephew come to Amsterdam as soon as possible.

"Uncle Mathias said he has something he wants to give me," Hector had told the girls after he got off the phone that day. "Something that he simply can't mail, under any circumstances. Then he went on and on about some crazy treasure hunt."

Hector looked solemnly at the girls. "Frankly, he didn't make much sense." He shook his head worriedly. "Uncle Mathias is getting on in years. He's always been a tad eccentric. And now, well, I think he might be unravelling . . . just a little."

Hector's uncle Mathias was the eldest brother of Hector's mother, Anneke De Vries. Mrs De Vries was billed with the Trimoni Circus as Anneke the Woodland Fairy. She performed amazing acts of winged gymnastics on the high wire.

The twins had met Hector's uncle once before when he had visited them at the circus. The girls had been five at the time and didn't remember much about him, other than the intricate set of doll's house furniture from Holland he had given them.

As Hector made plans to visit his uncle, the girls schemed to go along, too.

"We can use the offer Professor Finkleroy gave us in Baltimore," Beezel proposed to Hector. "He has a Merlin Hotel in Amsterdam. He said if we perform our magic act there, he'll pay for our flights *and* our rooms."

"Let us come with you, Hector," Mimi pleaded. "Professor Finkleroy already said it would be great!"

"Well," Hector said as he reviewed the calendar tacked to the inside of his circus trailer, "your parents are planning on going to Katmandu soon . . ." He turned and wagged his finger at them. "You'd have to leave the Changing Coin here. Remember what happened with the Great Paparella? The last thing we need is to lose it in a foreign country."

Beezel thought about the Changing Coin, and how much it meant to her and Mimi. Their good friend Simon Serafin, the Strong Man of the Trimoni Circus, had given the coin and its magic to them before he died. A few months ago, a magician named the Great Paparella had challenged the twins to a Magic Duel in Baltimore. Instead, he had stolen their coin—and almost stolen their magic as well. They had gone through a lot to get it back.

"We'll leave the coin here," Mimi said, nodding vigorously. "Safe at home with the circus. Right, Beez?"

"Absolutely!" Beezel agreed.

Even though the twins didn't need to have the coin with them to use its magic, they could never pass the magic on to someone else without it. In the future, when the time came to pass it on, the girls would have to touch the Changing Coin, and the person receiving the magic gift would touch it as well. Only then would the twins say the five magic words out loud. The magic would leave Beezel and Mimi and enter the other person.

Hector eyed the twins. "I suppose, if your parents say it's okay. But you'd have to promise to mind me, keep up with your lessons and not get into any of your ka-poofing messes—"

"We promise!" Beezel interrupted.

Once Mr and Mrs Trimoni gave their permission, it was settled. While Hector visited his uncle, the

8

twins would perform their magic act in Amsterdam's Merlin Hotel for two weekends.

Hector's uncle lived in the bottom floor of a house nestled next to the Prinsengracht, a canal in the old part of Amsterdam. When Hector and the twins arrived at his house, Beezel noticed two things. The first was a large display window full of doll's furniture. The second was a bright red door with a sign on it.

It said HOOGABOOM'S ORIGINELE POPPENHUIZEN.

"I think that means 'Hoogaboom's Original Dollhouses,'" Beezel said as she consulted her Dutch pocket dictionary.

"That's right," Hector said as he turned to face the twins. "Well, my uncle said he'd be here, so let's see." He opened the door and a bell above it jingled. Hector stood in the doorway and called out, "Uncle Hoogaboom! It's Hector!"

After a minute's wait, an elderly gentleman emerged from a back room and padded his way across the shop towards them. First in Dutch and then in fluent English, Mathias Hoogaboom greeted them warmly and hugged his nephew.

Beezel said, "It's nice to see you again, Mr Hoogaboom."

Hector's uncle frowned. "No, no, that just won't do." He scratched his beard and smiled. "You must call me *Uncle* Hoogaboom."

Tall and thin, with wispy white hair neatly combed back and a small beard centred on his chin, Uncle Hoogaboom looked more like a scientist than a man who built the tiny worlds that crowded the rooms of his shop.

He wore a long cotton coat with large front pockets. Beezel noticed they were filled with odds and ends. A magnifying glass and a pair of tweezers jutted out of one. String and some sort of wire dangled from the other.

"You must be tired from your flight," Uncle Hoogaboom said. "Come inside. I'll make some tea." He carried in one of their bags and set it on the floor. "It's so nice to have a visit from my favourite nephew."

"Uncle, I'm your *only* nephew," Hector said as he brought in the rest of their luggage.

"So you are." Uncle Hoogaboom laughed. "And how is my little sister?"

"Mom? She's just fine," Hector said.

Uncle Hoogaboom turned his attention to the twins. "Your parents are well?" The twins nodded.

"And you two have come here to perform at the Merlin Hotel."

"Professor Finkleroy owns the Merlin Hotels," said Beezel. "He saw our magic show in Baltimore and liked it."

What Beezel didn't mention was that she and Mimi used *real* ka-poofing magic in their show as well as stage magic.

With the magic of the Changing Coin, the girls could change animals and people into other animals by thinking the five magic words in order, imagining the new animal and pointing at the animal they wished to change. Before he died, Simon had asked them to protect the magic of the coin and keep it a secret.

"And how is Mr Whaffle?" Uncle Hoogaboom asked. "Didn't Hector tell me he's gone back to throwing knives?"

"Mr Whaffle is great," Beezel said. Mr Whaffle had been the girls' tutor before Hector took over, but his first love was his job with the Trimoni Circus as a premier knife thrower. "He's been throwing perfectly for weeks now."

Uncle Hoogaboom tapped his chin with his finger. "Who else?" He snapped his fingers.

11

"Meredith the fortune-teller! Is she still with your circus?"

"She had left, but she's back now," Mimi said. "Meredith came out of retirement because she's engaged to Mr Whaffle."

Meredith was a clairvoyant. She had not only warned them about the Great Paparella, but had told the twins that there were two other magic coins somewhere in the world as well: the Shrinking Coin and the Mind-Reading Coin.

"Well, I think that's everyone I know from *your* home," Uncle Hoogaboom said to the girls. "Now let me show you around mine."

It was a curious little store that they had entered. To Beezel it seemed like a cross between a museum and a parts shop. In front of them was a room lined with honey-coloured shelves.

"What *are* these things?" Mimi asked him, pointing to the contents of the shelves.

"Ah," Hoogaboom said. "This is my own little *afdeling onderdelen*, my accessories department. It's where I sell the things that make my models unique. These tiny things I call my Hoogaboom *details*."

Beezel glanced at Mimi and shrugged. Uncle

12

Hoogaboom laughed and motioned for them to look around. Hundreds of tiny accessories filled the shelves that lined the walls. Beezel examined the contents stacked neatly on top of one. Miniature table lamps, pianos and credenzas were lined up right next to sofas and teddy bears.

"If it ever existed in a real home, the miniature is on one of my shelves somewhere," Hoogaboom assured them as he opened a door to his left and went inside. "Come!"

They stepped into a small entry.

"My apartment is down there," Uncle Hoogaboom said, pointing to the end of the hall. "But before we have our tea, let me show you something else." He walked past a stairway that led to the upper floors and stopped at a door on the right. He opened the door and switched on the light. "This is where I have my *poppenhuizen*. This is my doll's house room."

"Oh, Beezel, look," Mimi said.

Beezel peeked inside. "They're wonderful."

"You've been busy, Uncle," Hector said.

The doll's house room was filled with enchanting replicas of houses. They rested on wooden cases built to display the models at eye level. Although

13

they were miniatures of houses, they were quite large.

It seemed to Beezel that the two-story English manor house next to her was at least four feet tall, from its base to the top point of its roof, and more than four feet wide. The two front doors were the size of two paperback novels, placed side by side.

"Everything I make uses the same scale," Uncle Hoogaboom explained. "It's all just as it would be if everything were one twelfth its normal size."

Beezel smiled as she peeked inside. They really were charming. No detail had been forgotten in furnishing the models.

Uncle Hoogaboom reached beside the model next to Beezel and pushed a button. The lights inside the house came on, revealing more of the intricate interiors: brocade-covered sofas, gilded mirrors, mosaic tabletops, tiny glass vases filled with flowers.

"Now . . ." Uncle Hoogaboom turned and placed a hand on each twin's shoulder. "Would you like to look around the shop or have a cup of tea with Hector and me?"

"Look around," Mimi blurted out.

"If that's okay," Beezel quickly added.

"That's fine," Uncle Hoogaboom said. "You girls can look at the doll's houses and then each pick out one of my details to take home with you. My treat." He smiled warmly at them.

"Great!" Mimi said.

"Thank you," Beezel said.

"Come along, nephew. I have much to tell you during your stay." Uncle Hoogaboom pointed skywards and announced, "But first I want to tell you more about the hunt I've been on!" He marched off towards his apartment.

Hector glanced at the girls, shrugged and followed his uncle down the hall. Beezel and Mimi turned their attention to the doll's houses.

"This one is my favourite," Beezel said as she peered inside the English manor's front window. She saw movement from the corner of her eye. It was as if something had run across the parlour, just out of her vision.

Beezel blinked and rubbed her eyes. *I must be getting tired.* She looked again. This time she swore she saw a tiny man, about six inches tall, run up the stairs at the rear of the parlour.

She tried peeking in the house's front windows, but she couldn't see into the sides or back of the

15

model. Uncle Hoogaboom had so many doll's houses in the room, pushed right up against each other, that very little space was left between them.

She carefully opened the front double doors of the model and peered inside. She could see the bottom of the stairs leading up to the second storey. *That's where he went*, Beezel thought to herself. *Right up those stairs.*

CHAPTER THREE

You have jet lag," Mimi concluded after Beezel told her she had seen a tiny man inside the model.

"I do not," Beezel said. "Come on, ka-poof me into a mouse and let me take a look. I know I saw something. I want to go see what it was."

"Okay, but don't take too long," Mimi said as she peeked down Uncle Hoogaboom's hallway. "If Hector finds out we did this, he'll get really mad."

"I'll be quick."

That's when Beezel's day had stopped being normal. Mimi had ka-poofed Beezel into a small brown mouse and placed her inside the front doors of the English manor doll's house.

"I'll go watch for Hector," Mimi then said to her sister.

Beezel had scurried across the parlour, up the

stairs and through the open door at the top, intent on searching the unseen rooms in the back for the little person she thought she had seen. She had scampered across a library and was halfway down a hall when she heard a metallic tinkle.

When she ran back to the library to find out what the noise was, the cat had spotted her and given chase.

Of course, if Beezel had known that Uncle Hoogaboom had a cat that would follow her through the doll's house front doors, she wouldn't have asked Mimi to ka-poof her in the first place.

As Beezel stood next to Mimi in the doll's house room, she knew she was lucky to have come out of the experience in one piece—because Beezel had no ka-poofing power while she was changed into a mouse. No, she was sure that if Mimi hadn't ka-poofed the cat, it would have had her for dinner.

"I had to climb up on Uncle Hoogaboom's display table to get you. And it's a good thing I figured out that the roof of this house swings up," Mimi said as she lowered it back into place. "Look what else I found out." She pulled on the front right edge of the house. The entire front of the house pulled away as a hinged door, revealing the interior rooms.

"Well, I'll be Mandrake's monkey!" Beezel said. "I wish I'd known about that *before* you ka-poofed me." She was amazed at the craftsmanship. When the hinged door on the front of the doll's house was closed, you could hardly tell it was there.

"Oops, I'd better fix the kitty." Mimi inspected the snail she held in her other hand. "She must have crept in while I was looking down the hall." Mimi looked at Beezel accusingly. "But *you're* the one who left the doors to the doll's house open."

Beezel thought about reminding her sister that she was a *mouse* when she had gone through the front doors of the doll's house, but she decided it wasn't worth the effort.

"So if *I* hadn't heard her little bell, she would have gotten you for sure." Mimi gave a self-satisfied smile. "I ka-poofed her in midleap."

"Thanks." Beezel watched as Mimi set the snail down on the floor and ka-poofed it back into a cat. Now that she was her normal self again, Uncle Hoogaboom's cat appeared to be a rather small and highly confused house cat, instead of the fierce monster Beezel had just faced.

"Well? Did you see the little person? Was he dressed in green and wearing a pointed hat?" Mimi teased as she reached down and scratched the cat's ears.

"No, all I saw was that . . . *creature*." Beezel brushed her hair back with both hands. She was still out of breath from running away from that darn cat. How Mimi could be so chummy with something that had been seconds away from eating her own sister was beyond her.

After they had admired the rest of Uncle Hoogaboom's doll's houses, they walked back to the detail room. Beezel opened the door. She saw Hector standing stock-still just inside.

He must have finished having tea with his uncle, she thought to herself. *But what in the world is wrong with him?*

CHAPTER FOUR

What's up, Hector?" Mimi asked.

Beezel looked at him. They were almost the same height. The twins, having grown over the last year, were now just an inch or so taller than their tutor. One lock of Hector's thick white hair fell across his eyes. She reached over and brushed it aside. She waved her hand in front of his face.

"Hector? You okay?"

"Huh?" Hector seemed dazed.

The twins eyed each other and shrugged.

Beezel turned and followed his gaze. About twenty feet away, in the far corner of the room, a woman was talking to a man. Nothing astounding about that. But she knew what had stopped Hector dead in his tracks.

The woman looked exactly like him. *Well, it's not*

that she looks like him so much, Beezel corrected herself. *It's that she's small like he is.* The two actually were quite different from each other. Hector had brilliant white hair, even though he was only in his mid-forties. But his most interesting feature was his eyes. They were a pale pink. Beezel had always thought they were lovely.

The woman Hector was staring at was even shorter than he was, with curly brown hair that fell to her shoulders. She seemed to be about Hector's age, or maybe a little younger.

She was talking to an older man, tall with dark hair, greying at the temples. The man leaned over her as he spoke, as if he were questioning her about something. Beezel couldn't make out what they were talking about, and it wouldn't have mattered anyway, because they were speaking in Dutch.

The small woman shook her head, turned away from him with an irritated expression and began to stock a shelf.

The tall man pushed passed them and into the hallway that led to Uncle Hoogaboom's apartment and went up the stairs without a word.

Mimi nudged Hector. "Let's get closer to her," she whispered.

Beezel grabbed Hector's frozen arm and pulled him towards the woman.

"Stop," Hector whispered in protest. "What do I say to her?"

"Say hello," Beezel whispered. "Say good afternoon."

Mimi sauntered over to the woman and inspected the items on the shelf she was stocking.

The woman glanced up and smiled at Mimi. *"Goedemiddag."*

Beezel thought she had a nice face. Her nose was slightly turned up at the end, and she had a smattering of freckles across her cheeks. Her smile was genuine, and her hazel eyes were warm and friendly.

"Excuse me," Mimi said. "Do you speak English?"

"Yes," she said. "Can I help you?"

"Do you work here?" Mimi asked.

"Yes," she said. "I'm Mr Hoogaboom's assistant. I run the shop for him. So if there is something particular you are interested in, just let me know. My name is Gaidic."

"I'm Beezel." Beezel shook Gaidic's hand.

"And I'm Mimi," Mimi said. "And um, well, I

thought you should know, there's a cat in the doll's house room."

"Oh, that's Fieffie, Mr Hoogaboom's cat," Gaidic said. "He had a hard time finding such a tiny cat. We needed one that was light on her feet and could move around the details in the shop without damaging anything. The mice nibble the furniture. Our little Fieffie hunts the mice for us."

"No kidding," Beezel muttered to herself.

Mimi picked up a strand of her hair from the side of her face and twirled it. "Um, this is my good friend Hector." She pointed to the frozen Hector standing behind Beezel. "He's Uncle Hoogaboom's nephew. He wants to meet you."

Beezel winced. Subtlety was not Mimi's speciality.

The woman looked behind Beezel to Hector, and a surprised smile lit up her face.

"Well, hallo!" She put out her hand and Hector shook it. "It's nice to see a kindred spirit. I'm Gaidic."

"I'm . . . I'm . . . Hector," he said. Gaidic and Hector chatted briefly in Dutch, but then Hector put up his hand like a stop sign. "I'm afraid I'm a slow translator," he said.

"And I'm being rude to leave out these girls,"

Gaidic said, smiling at the twins. "I was saying how very nice it is for your uncle to have family come." Gaidic glanced towards the door that led to Uncle Hoogaboom's apartment. "I've worked for your uncle for five years now." She looked at each of them, as if trying to decide if she should or should not say something. "And I think Mathias . . . needs you here now."

"*Needs* me?" Hector asked.

"Yes," Gaidic said, "for a couple of reasons. That man who was just in here? He's been pestering your poor uncle for days. Maybe he'll leave him alone now that you're here."

"Is he one of Uncle Hoogaboom's friends?" asked Beezel.

"Edwin? Goodness, no," Gaidic said. "He's a cousin of Pieter's. Do you know about Pieter? Mathias's best friend who died?"

"He just now told me about him," Hector said.

"He was a nice man." Gaidic looked out the window and then turned her attention back to them. "Edwin came to visit not long after Pieter died. He's been staying upstairs." She pointed to the ceiling. "I think he was hoping to inherit something . . . I don't know. It's always questions, questions . . . and too much nosing about with him. It's not my business, I'm sure, it's just that I'm very fond of Mathias."

"I'll keep an eye on him while I'm here," Hector reassured her.

"And perhaps, the other thing . . . I shouldn't be telling you," Gaidic said. Her cheeks reddened slightly. "But I've been worried about Mathias."

"Why?" asked Beezel.

"He's been talking to himself more and more," Gaidic whispered.

Hector laughed nervously. "Don't worry. He's always done that."

"I know, I know." Gaidic leaned in conspiratorially. "But now he's acting like someone is *answering* him." She touched her forefinger to the side of her head and tapped it once. "I just wanted you to know this . . . how do you Americans say it? Giving a heads-up?"

While Hector assured Gaidic that Uncle Hoogaboom had always been eccentric, Beezel and Mimi wandered around the room and looked at the doll's house details.

"Look at him," Mimi whispered. "I think he's in love."

"Hmm?" Beezel was thinking about what Gaidic had told them. Talking to yourself was no big deal, but answering someone who wasn't there sure could be. She glanced at Gaidic and Hector. "She looks very nice. I hope she likes him."

After a few minutes, Hector beckoned to the girls to come over.

"I forgot to ask, did you get to see inside Mathias's doll's houses?" Gaidic asked them. "Did you know they open up?"

"They're amazing," Beezel said.

"Beezel thought she saw a leprechaun," Mimi added.

Beezel felt her cheeks get hot. "I didn't say it was a *leprechaun*."

"Oh, it's not a leprechaun," Gaidic said with a twinkle in her eye. "*They* live in Ireland. Here in Holland we have little people called *kabouters*." She smiled at Beezel. "But not to worry, they're friendly. Many people who come to see these models have said they too have seen a *kabouter*. Me, I think he likes living where everything . . ." She paused for a moment before continuing. "Where everything is the right *size* for him."

Gaidic elbowed Hector in the arm and whispered,

"Perhaps this is who your uncle has been talking to, eh?"

Hector laughed. "I wouldn't put it past him."

"Have you ever seen a *kabouter*?" Beezel asked her.

Gaidic nodded. "One night, when I was locking up, I thought I saw a tiny man running through the models." She laughed. "You want to know what else I thought I saw?"

"Yes," the twins said together.

"I thought I saw him carrying a flashlight!"

Hector, Gaidic and Mimi laughed and carried on for a while about a tiny man *needing* a tiny flashlight after dark, but Beezel's mind was somewhere else. She was remembering the tiny man who had run up the stairs of the doll's house.

Was it really a kabouter? *she thought to herself. Because I know I saw something.*

28

CHAPTER FIVE

Move over, I can't see out the window!" Mimi shoved against her twin.

Hector had called a cab from Hoogaboom's shop. "After this," he said, "we'll use the buses and trams. It'll save money." Once they had piled their luggage in the trunk, they were on their way to their hotel.

It was late afternoon and the busy streets were full of people, many on bicycles, heading home after a day's work.

"There it is!" Mimi slid across the seat to the other window, pinning Hector against the taxi door.

Beezel leaned across the seat to see. She let out a long whistle. "Walloping wizard whiskers," she said. "The Merlin Hotel." She grabbed Mimi's arm. "And we're going to perform our magic act there!"

The girls squealed and then began to bounce up and down on the taxi seat.

"Listen, ducks," Hector said. "Can we sit still for a few more minutes? I have a lot on my mind."

"Sorry, Hector," Mimi said.

As the taxi drew nearer to the hotel, Hector reminded the twins for the tenth time that day that even though they were in Amsterdam, and even though they had never set one big toe outside the United States in all their eleven years of life, they would still have to study and do homework.

Beezel knew Hector was trying his best to take over for Mr Whaffle, the girls' previous tutor.

"Sure, Hector, sure," Mimi said, patting Hector's shoulder. She pointed at the front of the hotel. "Look at the flags, Beezel!"

"Come along now," Hector said as he got out of the taxi. The girls followed him into a grand hotel lobby with marble floors and cut crystal chandeliers.

"Professor Finkleroy can decorate my house anytime," Mimi said as they stepped inside their hotel room. A lush ruby red bedspread was on the bed. Gold and red brocade curtains hung at the window.

"You don't have a house," Beezel reminded her. The girls lived in a trailer with their parents, the owners of the Trimoni Circus.

"I will when I'm a famous artist," Mimi said as she whirled around the room and fell across the double bed on her back. "If you're nice to me, I'll let you come visit."

"And if you're nice to me," Beezel said as she heaved their suitcases on to the luggage rack in the closet, "I'll stop by on my world tour."

Hector opened the door that connected the two suites. "Well, I'll be," he said. His room was just as opulent, done in shades of blue and gold, with a big four-poster bed covered in a satin bedspread.

"Your bed is *huge!*" Mimi hopped up from their bed, ran across their room, took a running leap and jumped on Hector's.

"I'll get lost in that." Hector smiled and set his suitcase down. "Now you girls get cleaned up. We'll have dinner with Uncle Hoogaboom and turn in early. Tomorrow is a big day. You'll have to rehearse for your show and get used to the stage."

Back in their room, Mimi and Beezel unpacked. Ten days. Right now it seemed like for ever to Beezel. But she knew it would go by quickly.

"Tomorrow I want to go sightseeing," she told Mimi. "I hope Hector will take us."

"Me, too," Mimi said. "We don't need to practise much for our show, do we?"

"Well," Beezel said. "Not too much. Just so we'll know where everything is. And we have to make sure all our props got here. And the animals we hired."

"Oh, that reminds me." Mimi reached inside her backpack and took out a small plastic container. Beezel noticed it had tiny holes punched in the lid.

Mimi popped off the lid and poured the contents into her palm. "There you are, sweetie," she said to the ladybird that crawled across her hand. She carefully set the bug on the carpet.

"Mimi," Beezel said. "Exactly *what* are you doing?"

"Nothing." Mimi pointed at the little bug on the floor. Ka-poof. A five-foot-long boa constrictor appeared in its place.

"Great suffering sawdust! Not *Gumdrop*!" Beezel moaned. Gumdrop was Mimi's favourite pet. She took the snake with her everywhere. Beezel wasn't going to tell Mimi, because it would hurt her feelings, but she had been looking forward to some

32

time without the big snake. The care and feeding of boa constrictors was something Beezel could live without. She shook her finger at her sister. "Mom said you couldn't take a snake on an airplane."

"Well . . ." Mimi smiled mischievously. "I didn't take a *snake* on the plane, now, did I?" She reached down and picked up Gumdrop. "Besides, I couldn't leave her at home." She petted the boa on her head.

"Oh, heavens no," Beezel muttered as she put her clothes in the dresser. "And exactly how do you plan on keeping a snake in a five-star hotel? You'll give the maid a heart attack and we'll get kicked out."

"I've figured it all out, smarty."

"Well, all I can say is you'd better not let Hector see her." Beezel zipped her empty suitcase shut and shoved it to the back of the closet. "Because he'll box her up and ship her home."

"Hector won't see her." Mimi set the snake on the corner of their bed. "I'll just ka-poof her into something more . . ." She struggled for the right word. "More *manageable* when he comes in."

Beezel tilted her head to listen at their shared door. "Then you'd better ka-poof her right now," she whispered, "because I think I hear Hector coming."

Mimi pointed at the snake. Ka-poof. Gumdrop was a ladybird again just in time, because Hector tapped once on the door and opened it. Mimi nervously eyed the ladybird as it edged along the bedspread towards the corner of the bed.

"Listen, ducks," Hector said as he entered the room. "I've been thinking. Before we go out, I need to talk to you about my uncle."

Beezel looked at his face. He seemed worried about something.

"Is he okay?" she asked. "Did something happen?"

"No, no," Hector said. "But I had the strangest conversation while we were in his apartment today. My uncle talked to me about Pieter, his good friend that Gaidic mentioned, the one who died a few months ago. Pieter owned the building that Uncle Hoogaboom lives in. He lived on the second floor, above Uncle Hoogaboom. They spent a lot of time building models together in Uncle Hoogaboom's studio, he told me."

Hector coughed. "But here's the thing. Uncle Mathias said they were on a treasure hunt." Hector ran his hand over his face. "And this is the weird part." He stared at the twins. "He said it's the treasure from some Spanish galleon. *And* he said

34

that all the treasure from that ship is still hidden somewhere in Pieter's house. In the very house my uncle lives in."

"Well, maybe it is," Mimi said. "Maybe it's in an old chest up in the attic or something."

"It is possible, Hector," Beezel said. "Isn't it?"

"Wait, it gets worse," Hector said sadly. "He said he and Pieter had been looking for the treasure for twenty years."

"Twenty *years*?" Mimi said. "Heck, they should have found *something* by now! A gold coin at least."

"That is a long time," Beezel agreed.

Hector sighed. "I'm wondering if having his best friend die hasn't been too great a blow. Maybe it's confused things in his head. So tonight, if Uncle Hoogaboom starts prattling on about treasure, just humor him and change the subject." He nodded and smiled at the girls. "Well, enough of that. Let me see you two."

Hector leaned against the bed and eyed the twins from head to toe. "Aren't you going to change for dinner?"

Beezel nodded as she tried hard not to stare at the bed. Where was Gumdrop? Hector was almost *sitting* on the corner of their bed.

Mimi's eyes widened as they darted back and forth from Hector to the bedspread.

"Well," Hector said, "let's get a move on. I'm starving. My uncle said he is taking us to a nice café right around the corner." He pushed off the mattress and stood up. "I'll meet you girls down in the lobby."

"Okay," Beezel managed to say.

Mimi had covered her mouth in horror.

As soon as the door to their room closed, the girls rushed to the corner of the bed.

"Gumdrop!" Mimi cried as she searched for her.

"Did he?" Beezel couldn't bring herself to say it. What if Hector had smashed Gumdrop when he leaned against the bed?

CHAPTER SIX

Here she is!" Mimi sighed with relief. The little bug had begun to crawl down the foot of the bed towards the floor.

"Whew, that was a close call," Beezel said.

After they had changed, Mimi put the bug inside the plastic container and popped the lid back on. "I think I'll leave her in here until we get back from dinner."

"I think that's a good idea," Beezel said as she grabbed two sweaters, one for her and one for her sister.

The girls went down the stairs to the hotel lobby. Beezel saw Uncle Hoogaboom and Hector sitting across from each other by the fireplace. When Hector saw them, he stood up and waved.

"Hello there," Hector said to them. "You both look very nice."

Mrs Trimoni had sewn the girls new dresses for their trip. The one Mimi had picked to wear to dinner was made from a bolt of silk Siyan the Snake Charmer had sent the circus from China. Her dress was green with a flowing skirt that swirled when Mimi turned.

Beezel's dress was made from a sari covered in a pattern of lush red and brown flowers. Her dress fit her like a glove.

"Good and hungry, I hope?" Hector asked.

"You'll need to put on those sweaters," Uncle Hoogaboom said. "It's chilly outside." Beezel noticed that he had dressed up for their dinner as well. Gone was the long lab coat. It had been replaced by a tweed jacket over a shirt and tie. His pockets, however, were still packed to bulging. A pair of pliers peeked out from one.

On the way to the café, Uncle Hoogaboom said, "I've invited a young friend of mine to join us. I hope you don't mind. We're working on finding the treasure together." He put his finger to his lips and said to the girls. "Just between us, mind you!" Then he winked.

Beezel started to ask Uncle Hoogaboom what he meant, but she remembered what Hector had told them back in their room.

"Any friend of yours is a friend of mine, Uncle," Hector said quickly.

"You'll like Wiliken—he's a fine young man," Uncle Hoogaboom continued. "My friend Pieter, the one I told you about, Hector? Well, his son was Wiliken's father. He died a few years back. And then Pieter died not too long ago."

"Oh, that's sad," Beezel said.

Uncle Hoogaboom nodded in agreement. "Young Wiliken grew up in the States with his mother. He's come home to Amsterdam to settle things. I promised his mother I'd keep an eye on him while he's here." He shook his head sadly. "He didn't see much of Pieter, his grandfather." He sighed. "The boy doesn't even speak Dutch, except for *hallo* and *dag*." He looked at the girls. "Hello and goodbye."

They approached a café and Uncle Hoogaboom opened the door. "Here we are," he said. "Let's see if Wiliken has secured a table for us."

The small dark restaurant was lit by the warm glow of amber table lamps. Against the sides of the room, upholstered benches flanked oak tables, creating cosy nooks for talking and eating.

Uncle Hoogaboom scanned the room. "He's not here yet. We'll start without him; he won't mind." As he chose a table and sat down, he said, "The *broodjes* are very good here." He looked at the twins and smiled. "Those are sandwiches."

They ordered their *broodjes*, and their food arrived. Still Uncle Hoogaboom's friend had not appeared.

"Should we wait for him?" Hector asked, sandwich in hand.

"No," Uncle Hoogaboom said as he prepared to take a bite. "He should have been on time."

They had no sooner begun to eat than a young man, dressed in black, rushed up to their table.

Beezel took a quick glimpse at him. He looked like a teenager, although it was hard to tell. He was wearing a blue knit ski cap pulled down over his ears, dark glasses and a black jacket.

The young man whipped off his sunglasses. "Can't see a darn thing with these on," he said. "Sorry I'm late, Hoogaboom. He was after me again."

"Did you take the route I told you to?" Uncle Hoogaboom sounded like a teacher reprimanding a tardy student. "He wouldn't have found you if you had." He made a "tsking" sound and turned his attention back to his food.

"He saw me as soon as I left the lawyer's office," the young man said. "I had a heck of a time losing him." He stood staring down at them expectantly. Beezel realised there was nowhere for him to sit, but she was trapped on the other side of Hector. She elbowed him.

Hector must have understood her nudge because he rather reluctantly set down his sandwich and stood up. "I'll grab an empty chair from that table. You sit next to Beezel."

"Thanks," he said to Hector. He flashed Beezel a grin as he sat down next to her.

Beezel had a funny feeling she had seen that grin somewhere before, but she couldn't place it. She concentrated on cutting her sandwich in half.

From the corner of her eye, she saw him take off his jacket and ski cap and set them on the bench between them.

"So," Hector said as he put the chair at the end of the table and sat down. "Who's after you?" He took another bite of his sandwich.

"Blasted treasure hunters," Uncle Hoogaboom hissed.

Wiliken laughed. "Not this time!"

Beezel quickly glanced at Hector. He rolled his eyes and put one hand to his forehead. She bet he was thinking that his favourite uncle had officially unravelled a little bit more. She took a bite of her sandwich and glanced across the table at her sister.

Mimi's mouth was wide open, gaping as if she had seen a ghost.

"What's wrong?" Beezel asked, suddenly alarmed.

"You're . . . you're . . ." Mimi pointed at the young man sitting next to Beezel. "Wil Riebeeck!"

Uncle Hoogaboom glanced up from his meal. "Oh, I beg your pardon. Girls, Hector, this is Wiliken Riebeeck. Wiliken, next to you is Beezel. This is Mimi next to me, and this—" he pointed to Hector—"is my nephew, Hector."

Wil Riebeeck? Had she heard Mimi correctly? The expression on Mimi's face said she had. She hadn't really looked him directly in the face yet. Beezel slowly turned and stared at the young man next to her.

"Hi!" Wiliken said as he put out his hand. "Hoogaboom says you guys are from the States. Me, too. Welcome to Amsterdam." He smiled and shook each of their hands.

42

"You're Wil Riebeeck?" Mimi said dreamily. "*The* Wil Riebeeck? From the movies?"

"Yes." He laughed. "I guess I am. But around here, I'm just plain old Wiliken."

"Dear me, I forgot that you girls might know him as Wil Riebeeck, the renowned American movie star!" Uncle Hoogaboom said with a chuckle.

"Huh," Beezel stuttered. "Hi," she managed to squeak out.

She couldn't believe it. Uncle Hoogaboom's Wiliken was Wil Riebeeck, the famous actor! And he was sitting right next to her!

I sure hope I don't faint, Beezel thought to herself.

Wil Riebeeck had been in two blockbuster movies in the last year alone. His picture had been splattered on every tabloid and teen magazine she'd seen. But it was more than his acting that appealed to his fans. Even though he was only seventeen years old, Wil Riebeeck liked to go on dangerous adventures and frequently invited members of the press to come along. Beezel had often wondered if he did so with the hope that a few of the paparazzi would fall into the Amazon River, or tumble down Mount Everest and leave him alone.

"Wow," Mimi gushed as she stared at him. "You're *so* much cuter in person."

"Uh, thanks." Wiliken pulled at the collar of his sweater as he scanned the menu. Beezel thought he was holding it a little higher than he needed to. It almost covered his face. "Maybe you can order for me, Hoogaboom?"

Uncle Hoogaboom nodded.

Try as she might, Beezel found it hard not to stare at him. She had never seen a famous person before. Sure, the Trimoni Circus back home was full of interesting characters, and plenty of them were completely unforgettable, but none of them was famous all over the world. This one was. This one had long blond hair and green eyes. His skin was a golden brown, perfectly set off by the white pullover sweater he was wearing.

"So you're an actor?" Hector asked after Uncle Hoogaboom ordered Wiliken's dinner.

"Yeah, I guess you could say that." Wiliken smiled again. Beezel caught herself in midsigh. She coughed, in what she hoped was a delicate way, instead.

"I think I forgot to tell you, Hector . . ." Uncle Hoogaboom wiped his mouth with his napkin.

"Wiliken's grandfather owned a shipping company here. Been in shipping a long, long time, right, Wiliken?"

Wiliken nodded. "*Long* isn't the word for it. It's been in the family for more than three hundred years."

"That's right," Uncle Hoogaboom said. "And while Wiliken is here settling things, we're going to find some treasure."

Hector, Beezel and Mimi stopped eating in midbite. They stared at Uncle Hoogaboom, then at Wiliken.

Wiliken nodded in agreement, just as if all Uncle Hoogaboom had done was suggest having coffee after dinner. Then he turned to Beezel and said, "I hear you and your sister are amazing magicians. What kind of magic do you do?"

Beezel didn't know what to say. She wanted to ask about the treasure, but Hector had told her not to. Besides, Wil Riebeeck had actually asked *her* a question! And his incredibly green eyes were fixed intently on hers. So she tried to answer him.

"Um . . . uh . . . we . . . uh . . ." Beezel's starstruck nerves were back in force. She had the strangest sensation that her vocal cords were tied in a knot.

"We do all kinds, don't we, Beez?" Mimi chimed in. "I like illusions best."

They chatted about magic and the Trimoni Circus for a while. Beezel noticed Hector glancing often at his uncle with a worried expression.

Uncle Hoogaboom seemed to be enjoying himself thoroughly. Then at nine o'clock, as if a bell had gone off in his head, he stood up and announced, "*Lieve hemel!* It's time to go home."

Hector, Wiliken, Beezel and Mimi quickly gathered their things and followed Uncle Hoogaboom to the front of the restaurant. Uncle Hoogaboom insisted on paying.

"Thank you so much, Uncle Hoogaboom," Beezel said.

"It was delicious," Mimi added. "I'm stuffed."

"*Van harte welkom.* Glad you enjoyed it," Uncle Hoogaboom said. "Wiliken and I will see you to your hotel and take a bus home from there."

"Oh, are you staying near my uncle?" Hector asked Wiliken as they walked.

"*Very* near," Wiliken said as he pulled his ski cap

down to cover his blond hair. "Right now I live above him in my grandfather's apartment."

They came to the front steps of the Merlin Hotel. Uncle Hoogaboom wished them all good-night.

"It was very nice to meet you all," Wiliken said. He turned to face the twins. "As for you two, I'll see you tomorrow night."

"Tomorrow night?" Beezel said.

"Yes," Wiliken said. "I'm looking forward to your opening night."

"You're coming to *our* show?" Mimi asked him.

"I wouldn't miss it," Wiliken said. "As a matter of fact, I'm coming with Hoogaboom."

Uncle Hoogaboom glanced at his watch. "Come along, Wiliken. And keep your eyes sharp. Watch out for you-know-who."

"Not to worry," Wiliken said, affectionately patting the old man on the back. "I'll keep an eye out."

Mimi stared openmouthed as they walked away. "Beezel, Wil Riebeeck is going to be at our opening night."

"Looks like it." Beezel put her hand to her chest. As she watched the young man stride confidently

47

down the street with Uncle Hoogaboom, she noticed something. Her heart was beating just as hard as it had been when Fieffie the cat was about to eat her.

CHAPTER SEVEN

Why don't you finish your math worksheets before we go down to set up for your show?" Hector said to the twins the next morning as he studied their trip schedule. The three had eaten breakfast in the hotel restaurant and come back up to the twins' room to plan their morning.

"No! Please, anything but that!" Mimi groaned.

"Listen, my little termites," Hector said as he handed the girls their workbooks. "You're going to want to go see *all* the sights next week. The more work we do this morning, the less we'll have to do then."

Beezel grabbed a pencil and read the first problem.

If Josie had two chickens that laid thirteen eggs, and Nick had five chickens that laid four eggs, and their mother insisted they make three-egg omelettes . . .

"What could he be thinking?" Hector mused as he leaned back in the easy chair in the corner of the girls' hotel room. "An entire ship's treasure is inside Pieter Riebeeck's house and they haven't found it in twenty years? Humph!" He snorted in disbelief.

Beezel erased the answer she had written down. She read the problem over carefully and began to work out again just how many omelettes' worth of eggs those chickens had laid.

"I suppose it happens as you get older," Hector announced to no one in particular. "I've read that eventually your brain cells just start jumping off the high dive, one by one."

Beezel erased her answer again. Forty-two omelettes couldn't be right. She sighed and watched Hector for a moment. He closed his eyes and looked like he was going to take a nap. She began to work out the number of omelettes again.

"He's really cute, isn't he?" Mimi interrupted Beezel's egg count. "I mean, he's taken cuteness to a whole new level. Like if Wiliken's cute factor were in my math problem, the answer would be one billion."

Beezel rubbed her hands over her face. If Mimi said Wiliken Riebeeck was cute one more time, she was quite sure her head would explode. Mimi had managed to work it into the conversation four times after dinner last night and twice since she woke up. One more time, and Beezel would erupt. She *knew* he was cute. Any animal, including snakes, would look at Wiliken Riebeeck and know he was cute. She didn't need her sister to keep reminding her.

Beezel glanced at Mimi's worksheet. She had drawn three little hearts at the top. Inside each one Mimi had written *Wil*. Beezel felt a tiny pang and had a sudden urge to reach over and cross them out. Instead, she forced herself to think about omelettes again.

The twins worked quietly for a few minutes. Beezel finished her worksheet and waited for Mimi to finish hers.

"Done!" Mimi announced as she slammed her workbook shut.

"What *am* I going to do about my uncle?" Hector suddenly blurted out from the corner. "He's all alone now, except for Gaidic. I don't think Wiliken will stay in Amsterdam long." He sighed.

Beezel put her workbook on the dresser. "Why don't you go call him, Hector? Mimi and I can go downstairs and set up for tonight."

Hector studied them suspiciously. "You'll stay inside the theatre? I don't want to have to comb the hotel searching for you."

"We promise!" Mimi plonked her workbook down on top of Beezel's. She grabbed her backpack and slipped it on.

Beezel eyed the backpack. It was as much a part of Mimi as her short hair and bouncy nature. Mimi kept all her art supplies inside it and took it with her everywhere. But Beezel had a feeling there was a certain reptile among the art pens in Mimi's backpack this morning.

"Are you sure you have *everything*?" Beezel asked her sister sarcastically.

"Yep, I'm sure!" Mimi smiled at her and winked. "Well, come on, Beezel!"

Hector stood up. "I'll be right down. I just want to see if I can talk some sense into him."

The twins walked down the stairs and into the theatre where they would perform their magic act that night. Beezel and Mimi went backstage and located all the props that had been shipped from home. Carefully they set them up on the stage.

Back home, the girls had their beloved animals in the Trimoni Circus to use in their act, but bringing animals across the Atlantic Ocean for just ten days was impractical. Before they'd left, the Trimonis had found a man in Amsterdam who was willing to let the girls hire some animals from his petting zoo.

"The man with the animals we hired is coming at six," Beezel said. "I told him we didn't want any animals that bit or spooked easily. He said no problem, he has two old sheep he'll bring us to use in our show."

Mimi had ka-poofed Gumdrop back into a snake last night, and the boa had slept in the bottom drawer of their dresser in spite of Beezel's objections. Today, Mimi had ka-poofed Gumdrop into a ladybird again and smuggled her into the theatre inside her backpack. Now Mimi had changed her into a wallaby that was hopping up and down the aisles.

"Mimi, Gumdrop is getting away!" Beezel yelled at her sister. She pointed at the wallaby. Ka-poof. Gumdrop was a tortoise.

"She's just getting a little exercise," Mimi said. "She can't get much being a ladybird cooped up in that little plastic container."

Beezel shook her head. She considered reminding Mimi that *she* was the one who had put her in the plastic container in the first place. But most of the time, it really wasn't worth arguing with Mimi about anything. And especially not about animals. "Listen, Mimi, you've got to figure out something besides that plastic container to keep her in. You can't keep her as a ladybird."

"You're right," Mimi answered. "It's time for Operation GAAD to go into action."

"I know I'm going to regret this," Beezel said, "but what exactly is Operation GAAD?"

"Gumdrop As A Dog, of course." Mimi pointed to Gumdrop. Ka-poof. Gumdrop was an adorable white poodle. Mimi reached into her backpack and pulled out a pink dog collar with a silver heart dangling from it.

"You're kidding," Beezel said.

"I told you I had it all planned out," Mimi said as she fastened the dog collar around Gumdrop's neck. "And I brought kibble and a chew toy for her. I checked the contract Professor Finkleroy sent us before we left, and it said the Merlin Hotel lets you keep animals in your room if they are part of your act." She waved her hand at Gumdrop. "Ta da! The Amazing Gumdrop!"

Gumdrop the poodle seemed unimpressed. She yawned and curled up on the stage floor.

"Mimi," Beezel said, "Hector will be here any minute."

"Not a problem," Mimi said. "The contract said all I had to do was find the prop manager, a lady named Enid Something-or-other. It said she'll take care of our animals during the day." Mimi frowned. "She does charge extra for dog walks, but I'll figure that out later."

"Wouldn't it have been easier to leave Gumdrop home?" Beezel asked.

"No," Mimi said. "I just know Gumdrop wanted to come to Amsterdam, too."

The girls located Enid the prop manager in a small office backstage and introduced her to Gumdrop. They were happy to find out that Enid, like most Amsterdammers, spoke English as well as they did.

"What a cute little doggie," Enid said as she knelt down to pet Gumdrop. "We're going to have lots of fun!"

Gumdrop stared up at the young woman, opened her mouth and made a peculiar retching sound.

Beezel leaned over to Mimi and whispered in her

ear, "I think she's trying to hiss at her." Mimi nodded and, noting Enid's horrified expression, said, "She's okay, Enid, she just doesn't bark very well."

The twins assured her that they would retrieve Gumdrop long before their show started. As they walked away, Beezel turned and saw Enid gingerly pick up the hissing dog and carry it back towards the prop room.

When Hector came down to the theatre, the girls did a walk-through of their show. As they practised their finale, he seemed satisfied.

"How's Uncle Hoogaboom?" Beezel asked as they sat in the back seats of the theatre and looked down at the stage. "Is he okay?"

Hector shook his head. "He's absolutely convinced there's a treasure. He said he's very close to finding it, I'm not to worry and everything will make sense in a few days." He threw his hands up in the air. "Then he went on about something he has to give to me before I leave."

"Did you talk to Gaidic?" Mimi asked, smiling.

"Just for a minute." Hector smiled back. "She is nice, isn't she?"

The twins agreed.

"I'm glad you like her," Hector said. "I've asked her to come sightseeing with us sometime while we're here."

Beezel nudged Mimi and they giggled. "That's nice, Hector," Beezel said.

"Oh," Hector said as he examined his fingernails. "Gaidic had a good idea."

"What?" asked Mimi.

"She said since Wiliken is visiting, we should ask him to come along as well."

The twins looked wide-eyed at each other. Wil Riebeeck was going to go sightseeing with them?

"Great wands and rabbits!" Beezel said.

"You can say that again," Mimi said.

CHAPTER EIGHT

Mimi had never been nervous before on an opening night. Beezel couldn't tell if it was because they were in a foreign country, or because Wil Riebeeck would be sitting in the audience watching them. She found herself in the strange position of trying to get her sister to relax.

"Mimi, we'll do great," Beezel said as she applied her stage makeup. She outlined her blue eyes with charcoal grey eyeliner, dusted pink blush on her cheeks and then dabbed on some rose-coloured lip gloss with her finger. "Just remember, we've done these tricks a million times before."

"But we've always used our own animals before, Beez," Mimi whispered to her as she twirled her hair around her finger and brought the end into her mouth. "Tonight we have to use Hector and poor Gumdrop."

Beezel and Mimi had returned to the hotel at three o'clock that day, after visiting the Amsterdams Historisch Museum with Hector. The girls had waited and waited for the petting zoo man, but he had never shown up with his two sheep.

The twins had gotten Hector to agree to be one sheep for the show, and they secretly decided Gumdrop would have to be the other. They told Hector, however, that the other sheep was originally a fly Mimi had caught in their room that morning.

The twins had ka-poofed Hector and Gumdrop separately, and brought them together only after they had both been changed into sheep. The two of them were now quietly grazing on the shredded lettuce Beezel and Mimi had sprinkled on the floor of their dressing room.

Mimi eyed the two sheep nervously. "You know how Gumdrop can be when she's been ka-poofed for too long," she whispered. Beezel nodded.

Hector had been ka-poofed so many times, Beezel was quite sure he would be fine. But Gumdrop was another matter altogether. The boa appeared to have a one-track mind. All Gumdrop seemed to think about, no matter what animal form she took, was squeezing.

Beezel contemplated the two sheep and sighed. They'd just have to make the best of it.

For the most part, the show went well. The twins could see Wiliken sitting with Uncle Hoogaboom as they made their entrance on to the stage. Wiliken gave them a small wave and smiled. Mimi waved broadly back at him. Beezel smiled quickly and looked away before her heart could start its dance.

The girls flawlessly performed all the magic tricks they did without the animals. Then they did their favourite illusions: the Box of Doom, the Vanishing Twin and the Floating Fireballs. But the time came at last for the grand finale. It was time to use the ka-poofing magic on Hector and Gumdrop.

Beezel and Mimi brought the two sheep to the centre of the stage. Then the twins stood in back of them and looked at each other.

"I'm getting a little bored with having sheep, aren't you, Mimi?" Beezel said.

"You're so right, Beezel. We can do better." Mimi pointed at Gumdrop the sheep. Ka-poof. Gumdrop was a zebra. The crowd gasped.

"Oh, really. I think we can do better than that." Beezel pointed at Hector. Ka-poof. Hector was a hippopotamus. The crowd cheered.

"Too big, Beezel." Mimi pointed at Hector. Ka-poof. The hippo was an antelope.

"Well, so is yours." Beezel pointed at Gumdrop. Ka-poof. The zebra was a peacock.

The girls got a great reaction from the crowd each time they changed the animals. After several exotic animals appeared and changed in front of the audience's eyes, Beezel paused. Hector was now a llama. Gumdrop was a chimpanzee, tightly hugging Mimi around the waist as she held her on her hip.

"And now it's time to say goodnight." She pointed to Hector. Ka-poof. Hector changed from a llama into a small brown bunny.

The plan was for Mimi now to change Gumdrop into a bunny as well, and the twins would carry the rabbits off the stage. But Gumdrop had other ideas. Her eyes were riveted on Hector, the little rabbit.

"Uh-oh!" Mimi said as the chimp sprang from her arms and jumped across the stage. Gumdrop the chimp grabbed Hector the rabbit so quickly Beezel didn't have time to react. Gumdrop bounded off the stage and behind the curtain with the poor rabbit locked in her arms.

The crowd, thinking this was part of the act,

laughed and applauded. But Beezel knew what was running through Gumdrop's snakelike mind. Gumdrop had found dinner. Now she would find a nice quiet spot to squeeze the life out of the rabbit and eat it.

"Well, goodnight! Thank you!" Beezel yelled as she grabbed Mimi's hand and the two bolted from the stage. As they dashed down the backstage steps, the twins could hear the audience calling for an encore. But there would be no curtain calls for the Trimoni Twins tonight.

They had to find Hector before Gumdrop ate him.

CHAPTER NINE

Rushing down the cramped corridor behind the stage, the girls quickly peeked inside each of the dressing rooms, searching for Gumdrop and Hector. They managed to irritate several performers, one of whom threw a shoe at Mimi when she looked underneath her dressing table for the snake-turned-chimp.

"Where could she have gone?" Mimi huffed as they turned the corner and jogged towards the prop room. "She couldn't open the door into the hotel without dropping Hector first, could she?"

"I don't think . . ." Beezel was interrupted by a woman's bloodcurdling scream coming from the other side of the stage door that led into the hotel itself.

"Gumdrop!" the twins said together as they

pushed open the door and darted down the hotel hall.

"There!" Beezel pointed to a woman standing petrified at the other end of the hall. Sitting on the floor in front of the woman, holding a squirming brown bunny, was Gumdrop.

"Make it go away!" the woman sobbed as she pointed a shaky hand at the chimp.

"Keep still!" Mimi yelled at her. She pointed at the chimp. Ka-poof. Gumdrop changed from a chimp into a small white poodle. Hector tumbled to the floor and hopped quickly to the girls' side.

Mimi pointed at the brown bunny. Ka-poof. Hector was Hector again.

"I've never been so afraid in all my life!" Hector's face, although always extremely pale, seemed to have gone a light shade of grey. "I thought that chimp was going to strangle me for sure." He put his hands to his neck as if checking to make sure it was still there.

The woman at the end of the hall was beside herself with fear. She pointed at the twins now with the same shaky hand. "You . . . you . . . *changed* . . . it!" She backed up as she spoke. "That horrible monkey . . ." She gawked at Gumdrop. "It's a dog now . . . I saw you!"

64

Gumdrop the poodle gazed intently at the woman and made a sound that came out as something between a growl and a hiss. The woman squealed in panic.

Beezel sighed and turned to her sister. "Better get your watch." Mimi's amazing ability to hypnotise people had come in handy more than once before.

Mimi pulled Grandpa Trimoni's pocket watch from her sleeve and talked in a calming voice as she edged towards the hysterical woman. "You're fine," she said sweetly. "You're just fine." She continued to talk to the woman in soothing tones. As soon as the woman seemed to settle down, Mimi waved the watch in front of her face.

"You're getting sleepy," Mimi said.

"Sleepy?" the woman answered, as if not yet convinced.

"Yes," Mimi said. "Very, very, sleepy."

"Yes."

"You did not see anything in the hall tonight."

"Nothing in the hall," she murmured.

"You're tired and you'll get a good night's sleep."

"Umm." The woman smiled, eyes closed.

"*After* you go to your room," Mimi quickly added. "When I count to three, you will wake up. You won't remember anything that happened in the hall. You'll just want to go to bed and rest. One, two, three."

The woman opened her eyes and evaluated the scene in front of her.

Beezel stood next to Hector. The small white dog wove herself in and out of Mimi's legs.

"I hope you have permission to have that dog in the hotel," the woman announced as she gave them all a wide berth. "I will be speaking to the manager about this." Then she yawned and headed down the hall.

"Old bat," Mimi muttered.

"Come on, Hector," Beezel said. "You probably need to have a nice warm bath."

"And a nice warm drink," Hector said shakily. "I've never seen an animal with a look like the one that chimp had in her eyes. What did you say she was before you ka-poofed her? A fly?" He shook his head and eyed the dog. "Are you sure? No fly ever looked like that. That animal was going to eat me, bunny tail and all."

Beezel put her arm around Hector and glanced over her shoulder at Mimi. She watched as Mimi pointed at Gumdrop. Ka-poof. Gumdrop was a tiny grey mouse. Mimi quickly picked the mouse up by the tail and slipped it inside her front pocket.

No sooner had Beezel turned back around than she saw Wiliken Riebeeck running full tilt down the hall.

"They're right behind me!" Wiliken yelled as he got closer. "Which way is the exit?"

"Who?" Beezel asked, but then she saw them. A pack of paparazzi, cameras flashing, had turned the hallway corner and was headed their way.

The sight of the stampeding reporters brought Hector around. He shook his fist at them. "Dang-blasted press! Never there when you need 'em, always there when you don't!" Hector pushed Wiliken behind him. "Don't you worry, young man, I'll get rid of them," he said. "You girls take Wil backstage and hide him. I'll come tell you when the coast is clear."

Beezel grabbed Wiliken's hand. "Come on!"

Mimi pulled the stage door open. "Run!"

As they ran past the dressing rooms to the back of the stage, Beezel could hear Hector shouting at the reporters, "Stop right there! Only performers past this point! Security, over here!"

"Where can we hide him?" Mimi asked, out of breath.

"In here!" Beezel slid open a hidden panel on the Box of Doom. "You'll have to sit with your knees against your chest."

"Anything to get away from those guys," Wiliken said as he flashed her the grin she had seen so many times in movie theatres.

Suppressing the urge to sigh and stare at him, she pushed the edge of his jacket inside the box and slid the panel shut.

"Now be quiet and sit still," Mimi whispered to him.

Beezel and Mimi busily pretended to pack up their equipment.

A few minutes later one of the reporters burst into the room. He had orange frizzy hair, a round face and a round belly to match.

"Where did he go?" he demanded of the girls. He glanced over his shoulder. "Come on, come on! That shrimpy guy with the white hair will be here any minute." Seeing their mute faces, he said, "Don't you people speak English over here?"

"Yes," Mimi said sweetly, "as a matter of fact, we do."

"Listen up, little girls," the man said. "I'm a very important American reporter, so don't waste my time. I'm looking for Wil Riebeeck. And I know he came back here."

"We haven't seen him," Beezel said, smiling as innocently as she could.

The man eyed the Box of Doom. "What's in there?" he said, kicking the side of the box.

"Hey," Mimi said. "Don't kick our equipment!"

"Do you want to see inside?" Beezel turned and winked at Mimi.

The twins turned the box to face the reporter. Beezel slid open the front. It appeared to be empty.

"See?" Mimi said happily. "Nobody there!"

The man scrutinised them suspiciously. "Who are you two? Are you friends of Riebeeck's?"

"We," said Beezel as she put her arm around her sister, "are the amazing Trimoni Twins! Would you like to take a picture of us for the newspaper?"

"Ha! You're not in the same league as Riebeeck, sisters." He turned and began to inspect the Box of Doom, looking very carefully at its construction. Beezel decided she'd better distract him before he accidentally figured out its secret and deposited Wiliken on the floor in front of them.

"You must be an *amazing* reporter," she said as she elbowed Mimi. "How did you know that Wil Riebeeck was going to be here tonight?"

"Little girl, this is *nothing*. This is chump change," the reporter said inches from Beezel's face. She pretended not to notice his bad breath. "I've tracked Riebeeck all over the world."

"And I bet he's very hard to follow," Mimi added, stepping between the reporter and the box that hid Wiliken.

"Not so hard. He's given me the slip once or twice. But all in all, he's been a continual source of good income." He smiled slowly. "And I'm sure he'll be good for more." Beezel tried hard not to flinch. His two front teeth were tinged with grey. The ones on either side of them weren't looking too healthy either.

He leaned in close to the girls. Beezel held her breath. "Let me tell you something about this pretty boy star," he said. "I've got them lining up to give me dirt on the guy."

Beezel heard what sounded like a low growl coming from inside the Box of Doom.

"You know," she said rather loudly to drown out Wiliken, "I can't believe anyone would ever say anything bad about Wil Riebeeck. He seems like such a nice person."

"Believe me, there's always *someone* willing to talk for a price." The fat man had decided to clean his fingernails with a toothpick while he talked to them. "There's a guy staying at his house, someone in his family—he told me plenty about him, *and* about his grandfather." He snorted. "Wil Riebeeck's crazy old grandpa. That story alone made me a few thousand dollars. I sold it to an American magazine yesterday."

Mimi raised her arm and pointed at the reporter. Beezel quickly knocked her arm down. "Mimi," she scolded through clenched teeth, "it's not nice to point."

"I wasn't pointing," Mimi argued. "I was going to . . ." She looked at Beezel. "Never mind."

"Hey, pal!" The twins saw Hector standing on the edge of the stage. "I thought I escorted you out of the building. You're not allowed back there. It's strictly performers only. Do I need to call security again?"

"Keep your shirt on, squirt," the man said to Hector. He turned back to the twins. "Just remember, if you want to tell me some little story about him, or his family . . . or maybe you have a photograph of him? I pay good money. And I prefer they're not good stories, if you know what I mean."

He pulled a wallet out of his back pocket. "Get in touch with me next time you see star boy." He handed Beezel a card.

Hector jumped down from the stage and followed the reporter. "Finish packing," he told the twins, motioning with his head to the Box of Doom. "I'll see this guy out and be right back."

"That reporter is a complete sleazeball," Mimi said after they left.

"With bad breath," Beezel said.

"Oh my gosh!" Mimi said. "We forgot about Wil!" She turned the box around and opened the secret panel, and Wiliken climbed out. "Are you okay?" she asked him.

"I'm fine, but it was hard not to bust out of the box and punch that guy in the nose," he said.

"You can't do that," Beezel said as she handed him the reporter's card. "That's just what he wants you to do. Think of how he'd write *that* story."

"You're right." Wiliken smiled. "But, still, it's very tempting!" He glanced at the card. "I knew it was Slear. He follows me everywhere. That guy has made me his personal mission. I can't buy a slice of pizza without that jerk's face popping up."

"Do you know who it was that talked to him about your grandfather?" Beezel asked him.

Wiliken nodded. "I know exactly who it was. My grandpa's second cousin, Edwin."

Beezel and Mimi exchanged looks. Edwin was the name of the man Gaidic had told them about.

"He's a real pain," Wiliken said. "Hoogaboom said he was always dropping in on my grandpa uninvited for weeks at a time. As soon as grandpa died, he was at the front door, bags in hand, waiting to hear the will read. And he's *still* here. Hoogaboom says he's miffed that my grandpa left me the house instead of him." Wiliken shrugged sadly. "But I didn't think family did that sort of thing to each other, you know? Sold family stories?"

"They shouldn't," Beezel said. In the Trimoni Circus, their family and friends were the most important things they had. She couldn't imagine doing what Edwin had done.

"Yep, that Edwin guy is as big a jerk as Slear," Mimi said.

"Mimi!" Beezel said, glancing at Wiliken to see if

Mimi had offended him. After all, they were related. But Wiliken just laughed and agreed.

"Hoogaboom will hit the roof when he hears Edwin did this," Wiliken said. "He's been worried that Edwin is after our treasure. But at least he's leaving at the end of the week, and we'll be rid of him."

Mimi's mouth fell open.

"Great sorcerer's sweat socks!" Beezel said. "You mean to tell me that *you* think there's treasure inside your grandpa's house, too?"

"Of course," Wiliken said as he dusted off his pants. "Didn't Hoogaboom tell you we were looking for it? He told me he was going to."

"He did tell Hector," Mimi said. "But he said it was *all* the treasure from a Spanish galleon. And that *all* of it was hidden inside the house somewhere."

"*And* he said that he and your grandpa have been looking for it for *twenty* years," Beezel said.

Wiliken grew silent.

"Wil?" Mimi asked. "Are you okay?"

"Huh?" Wiliken said. "Oh, I was just thinking, and Hoogaboom is wrong."

Beezel's heart sank. Uncle Hoogaboom was

unravelling after all. The treasure was probably just some gold coins tucked away somewhere. Hector was going to be so upset when he found out.

"Yeah, he's dead wrong," Wiliken said thoughtfully. "I think it's been twenty-*two* years."

It was the twins' turn to be silent. Finally, Mimi said the thing that was on Beezel's mind as well. "But that's just crazy," Mimi said. "If there was all the treasure from a galleon inside the house and they had been searching for it all that time, they would have found it."

"Well, we are getting closer," Wiliken said cheerily.

Beezel and Mimi looked at each other. Beezel didn't know what to say. The twins stood motionless next to each other and stared at Wiliken.

"Hey . . ." Wiliken ran his hands through his hair. "I really enjoyed your show tonight. You guys are amazing."

Beezel managed a thanks. Did Wiliken actually believe what he was telling them? He seemed to. She didn't get a chance to ask him, because Hector had returned.

"Coast is clear, Wiliken," Hector said proudly. "I personally escorted each and every one of those guys out of the hotel. And the security guard is waiting for you in the hall. He's got a Merlin Hotel car parked by the kitchen door ready to take you back to your house."

"Thanks, Hector," Wiliken said. "I'm sorry about all this."

"Not a problem," Hector said. "I don't like their type one bit. It felt good to toss them out." He smiled and looked at the twins. "What's the matter with you two?"

"Nothing," Mimi said. "We're just thinking."

"Well," Wiliken said, "I should get going. Hoogaboom and I still want to do a little treasure hunting before we turn in."

As they stood and watched Wiliken leave to meet the security guard, Hector said to the girls, "Correct me if I'm wrong, bumblebees, but did Wiliken Riebeeck just say he was going on a treasure hunt?"

"Yep." Mimi nodded.

"He sure did," Beezel said.

"Then I guess my poor uncle isn't the only one unravelling a little bit, is he?" Hector shook his head and herded the girls back to their room.

CHAPTER TEN

Beezel, I've lost her," Mimi sobbed as she crawled across the floor the next morning. "Oh, poor, *poor* Gumdrop!"

"Stop crying, Mimi," Beezel said as she looked under their bed again for the missing snake. "We'll find her. It's not like it's the first time you've misplaced Gumdrop."

Mimi sniffed and wiped her eyes. "You're absolutely right, Beez. I just have to be logical about it, like you." She chewed on her lip. "Let's see. First, I got Gumdrop from Enid and took her up to our room. Then I fed her some kibble. Then I ka-poofed her into her old self again. . . ." She looked at Beezel. "Because Gumdrop can't be a dog all day—it makes her grumpy."

"Then we sat on the bed and looked at the guidebook," Beezel said. "And I took a shower."

"And then I went into Hector's room to ask if we could see Rembrandt's house this week . . ." Mimi froze.

The twins slowly stood up and stared across the bed to the door that separated their room from Hector's. It was wide open.

"MIMI!" The twins flinched as they heard Hector scream her name.

"Guess I'd better go explain," Mimi said in a small voice.

Beezel sighed. "I'll come with you."

Hector didn't wait until the twins were actually *inside* his room to begin yelling at them.

"You've actually smuggled a boa constrictor into the Merlin Hotel! In *Amsterdam!*" he shouted. "Of all the idiotic animal muddles you've cooked up, this one takes the cake!" He pointed to the big snake on the floor. "There are times when I think *Gumdrop* has more common sense!"

Hector ranted for a few more minutes, but when he saw tears welling up in Mimi's eyes, he caved. "Oh, don't cry, duck," he told her. "We'll figure something out."

"I already did, Hector." Mimi blew her nose on the tissue Beezel handed her and proceeded to tell

Hector all about Operation GAAD. "And Enid, the prop manager, takes care of her. She'll even take her for a walk if we want her to. I'll pay for everything with my allowance."

Hector rubbed his hands over his face, then stared down at the boa curled up at his feet. "Gumdrop. This is just what I needed. Well, it can't be helped. You get her downstairs now . . . as a *dog*." He shook his finger at Mimi. "And you leave her downstairs as a dog. Let the prop manager take care of her. I'll work out the details with her."

"Thank you, Hector." Mimi jumped up and kissed his cheek.

Beezel shook her head. She knew Mimi couldn't go two hours without checking on her snake. There was simply no way she would leave the big boa alone for several days.

That afternoon, Hector took the girls to the Van Gogh Museum. Beezel thought he did it because he was feeling a little guilty over his reaction to Gumdrop.

Mimi was thrilled to see the paintings of one of her favourite artists, Vincent Van Gogh. So thrilled that she spent the entire way back to the hotel making plans for her own art career.

"It's going to be so great, Beezel," Mimi said. "I'll have a studio, and I'll paint all day and all night. I'll be poor at first, and miserable. But then, someone will discover me, and I'll be fantastically rich! And Gumdrop and I will come visit you!" She twirled her hair thoughtfully. "Of course, it would be good to combine our visits with an art opening, wouldn't it?"

Beezel nodded.

"You're awfully quiet, duck," Hector said to her. "Are you feeling all right?"

"I'm fine," Beezel said. She wasn't sick; she just was remembering all the times she and her sister had practised their magic act together. Performing magic with Mimi always made her happy.

It was no different that night. The show went well and Beezel felt on top of the world. Mr Hendricks, the petting zoo man, finally found the hotel and brought two very docile sheep for the twins to use in their finale. Beezel was extremely thankful they did not have to use Gumdrop. And as she gazed out into the audience, she realised Hector wouldn't have been available either. He was sitting in the front row with Gaidic.

"He must have called her sometime today," she said to Mimi while they were taking their bows.

Once they were back in their rooms, Hector told them that he and Gaidic wanted to take the twins and Wiliken sightseeing the next day.

"Uncle Hoogaboom wants to come along as well. But if you want to go, you have to finish the first draft of the essay I assigned to you," Hector said, hands on his hips.

"Not 'How the Euro Is Different from the U.S. Dollar'!" Mimi moaned.

"I'll be back to check them in thirty minutes." He went back to his room.

Beezel and Mimi quickly wrote down everything they could think of about currency. Then they brushed their teeth and got into bed.

Hector came back in and reviewed the girls' work. Then he said, "By the way, Uncle Hooga-boom said he wants Wiliken and me to talk privately with him soon." He raised his eyebrows as he looked at the girls. "I have no idea what this is about, but the next time we're over for a visit, if you girls could help Gaidic in the shop, I'll find out."

Hector pulled the covers up over the twins and frowned. "But why in the world would my uncle want to talk to me and Wiliken *together*? I just met Wiliken." He sighed. "You don't suppose the two of them want to get me involved in their crazy treasure hunt, do you?"

Beezel didn't say anything, but she had a feeling that was exactly what they wanted.

When the twins woke up on Sunday, it was a glorious, sunny spring day.

"We don't have a show tonight!" Mimi said as she bounced on the bed.

"Mimi!" Beezel said. "Stop it! I'm getting seasick!"

After breakfast, Hector, Beezel and Mimi took Gumdrop the dog for a quick walk before depositing her back with Enid. Uncle Hoogaboom, Wiliken and Gaidic appeared in the lobby of the Merlin Hotel at ten o'clock sharp, and they set out for the day.

At Mimi's request, they went to see modern works of art at the Stedelijk Museum in the morning. They ate a quick lunch, and per Beezel's request, went on a canal boat tour in the afternoon.

Afterward they went for a walk down the Prinsengracht, the Prince's Canal.

"I wanted you to see my neighbourhood," Uncle Hoogaboom told the girls. "It is a very special place."

"I love it here," Beezel told him.

"It sure feels different from back home, doesn't it, Beezel?" Wiliken asked, and she agreed.

Uncle Hoogaboom explained that the canal dated back to the seventeenth century and that the beautiful homes that lined it were part of what was once the Golden Age of Amsterdam.

They strolled lazily along, and spent the afternoon popping in and out of the shops. When they passed a street named the Tuinstraat, Uncle Hoogaboom herded them into a little café for dinner followed by *appelgebak*, a delicious apple pastry. A few more houses down the street was Uncle Hoogaboom's shop on the ground floor of Wiliken's grandfather's house.

"There's one more place I want to show you." They walked past Uncle Hoogaboom and Wiliken's house to a wide street called the Westerstraat and then across to an old market square, called the Noordermarkt.

"There's a flea market here tomorrow," he told them. "You girls would love it. Hector, maybe you can bring them back here to do some more shopping?"

"Yes!" Beezel and Mimi said together.

Hector laughed. "All right."

Then Uncle Hoogaboom showed them the Noorderkerk, the North Church. Outside in the square, Beezel and Mimi fed bread crumbs to some birds and watched the sun beginning to set.

Beezel nudged Mimi and pointed to Hector. He and Gaidic were holding hands. The twins looked at each other and tried hard not to giggle.

"Should we head back?" Uncle Hoogaboom asked them after awhile. They all agreed that they were getting tired. Gaidic said goodbye and left for her bus stop.

"Uh-oh," Wiliken said as a black car drove in front of the square and slowed down.

Beezel saw a familiar round-bodied man with frizzy orange hair inside the car. "Isn't that Slear?"

"Great," Wiliken said. "Listen, I'm going to lose this guy and then I'll catch up with you, okay?"

"That's fine," Uncle Hoogaboom said as he pointed right, in the direction of their house. "We'll head home the long way, across the Violettenstraat.

You should go left, Wiliken. Head up the Boom-straat and cut over. We'll meet back at the house."

Wiliken rejoined their group after several blocks of outmanoeuvring Slear. "That guy just doesn't give up," he said, panting.

"We're almost home," Uncle Hoogaboom said. "Just a few more blocks. If that Mr Slear sets foot inside our home, I'm calling *de politie!*"

"That's the police," Hector whispered to the girls.

They walked quietly along the Violettenstraat together. The street was almost empty. Beezel looked at the houses and imagined each one had a family enjoying a cosy dinner inside. The thought made her homesick, and she wondered how her parents were doing in Katmandu.

The sound of a car screeching around the corner broke into her thoughts and got all of their attention.

"He should slow down," Wiliken said. "What a jerk."

"Oh no! Look!" Mimi pointed to a scruffy dog that had decided at that moment to pad across the street to greet them.

"Go back, doggie!" Mimi said softly.

The black car raced down the street towards

them, and towards the dog that seemed oblivious to the approaching danger. The dog ambled halfway across the street and sat down to scratch himself, smack bang in the path of the oncoming car.

Mimi raised her hand and pointed at the dog.

Oddly, at the same time, Uncle Hoogaboom raised his hand and pointed at the car.

Ka-poof! The dog was a clam.

Zuuft! The black car shrank to the size of a sandwich.

The pint-size car bumped into the clam and sent it spinning in circles, inches away from its bumper.

Mimi turned and stared wide-eyed at her sister. "Beezel! How in the heck did you do *that*?"

Beezel looked at Mimi. "Me? *I* didn't do anything!"

The girls turned and stared at Uncle Hoogaboom.

He smiled sheepishly at them and said, "I'm afraid that was me."

CHAPTER ELEVEN

You have the Shrinking Coin," Beezel proclaimed immediately. "I just know it."

"Yes," Uncle Hoogaboom confessed. "I do." He broke into a grin. "I call the magic zuufting. It makes that sound, don't you think?"

"We call ours ka-poofing for the same reason!" Mimi said. "Does the magic work like ours?" Without waiting for an answer she said, "Isn't this great, Beezel?"

Beezel nodded happily. It *was* great. She wasn't sure why it made her happy, but it did. It was good to know that the magic had stayed alive in two of the three coins. And somehow, knowing Uncle Hoogaboom had been given the same responsibility as the two of them made Beezel feel less alone. As if they had found a comrade of sorts.

"Uh, Hoogaboom," Wiliken said as he pointed to Mimi, "what did Mimi just do to that dog?"

"I do believe you've just witnessed the magic of the Changing Coin!" Uncle Hoogaboom said happily.

"You *know* about the Changing Coin?" Mimi said.

Uncle Hoogaboom nodded.

Beezel thought he seemed very pleased about things. She was just about to ask him how he knew about the Changing Coin when she thought of something. Wiliken hadn't reacted at all to Uncle Hoogaboom shrinking the black car. She turned to him. "You already knew about the Shrinking Coin, Wiliken?"

"Yep." Hector, Beezel and Mimi gawked at him. Wiliken laughed. "You should see your faces!"

"Well, well, we do have a lot to talk about, don't we?" Uncle Hoogaboom said as he gestured towards the centre of the road. "But first . . . Hector, perhaps you could get them out of the middle of the street. It's getting dark, and we don't want them to get run over."

Hector looked back and forth, and then ran to retrieve the clam and the car.

"Well, I'll be . . .," Hector said as he handed Mimi the clam and examined the outside of the tiny car. "My own uncle has had the Shrinking Coin all these years and . . ."

"Let me take care of this first, nephew, and then we'll chat," Uncle Hoogaboom said quietly. "In my experience I've found that if I un-zuuft someone fairly quickly, they are easily led to believe they've had a small accident of some kind, and as a result experienced a momentary loss of consciousness."

Uncle Hoogaboom set the car down by the kerb near a streetlight. "But I don't see the driver, do you?"

They knelt next to the little car and peered inside.

"Oh, I see him," Mimi said as she put her face against the back windshield. "There he is. He's hiding on the floor in the backseat."

The sight of a giant Mimi staring at him caused the tiny man to scramble back into the front seat.

"Hey, he looks kind of familiar," Mimi said.

"Merlin's magic meatballs!" Beezel said as she looked in the car and saw the man's orange hair and wide belly. "It's Slear!"

"Oh no," Wiliken said. "Not him. Please say it's not him."

"It's him," Hector said as he peered through the front windshield.

"He's mad," Beezel said.

The tiny man shook his fist and cursed at them from the driver's seat.

"Such language! Little man, there are young ladies present!" Uncle Hoogaboom scolded Slear. He turned to them. "Let's get this over with. You'll need to stand back."

They moved away from the little black car. Hector quickly surveyed the street. "The coast is clear."

Uncle Hoogaboom pointed. Zuuft. A full-sized car was parked in front of them.

"You've had a slight car accident," Uncle Hoogaboom said to Slear as he leaned inside the driver's window. "Are you all right?"

"That was no accident, pal," Slear yelled in his face, causing Uncle Hoogaboom to stand up and take a step back. "You . . . you *shrank* me! *And* this car!" Slear shot a look at Mimi. "And that kid changed a dog into a rock!"

"It was a clam," corrected Mimi.

Beezel elbowed her. "Shh!"

"Whatever it was," Slear said, "it was *real* honestto-goodness-presto-chango *magic!*" He spotted Wiliken standing behind Hector. "And you're in on it, aren't you, star boy?"

"Please stop calling me that," Wiliken said through clenched teeth.

Slear ignored him. "Finally! I've hit the jackpot! Ka-ching!" He let out a war whoop. "I'm going to have plenty to say about this, you can bet your life!" Slear grinned at them.

"He *looks* as happy as a clam," Hector muttered.

"Mimi, you'd better get your watch," Beezel said. She whispered to Uncle Hoogaboom, "Mimi's a great hypnotist."

"That must come in very handy," Uncle Hoogaboom said thoughtfully.

Mimi reached inside her sleeve to get Grandpa Trimoni's watch. She waved it at Slear. "You are getting sleepy," she said.

"Oh no I'm *not*," Slear said. "You're not taking this story from me, sister!" He grabbed a camera from a bag on the seat next to him.

"Mimi, it's not working," Beezel said nervously.

"Some people are more difficult to convince than others," Uncle Hoogaboom said. "I'll zuuft him again. We'll take him home until we can think of something." He sighed as he lifted his arm to point at Slear.

"Oh no you don't!" Slear thrust a camera out the car window and pointed the camera's flash at Uncle Hoogaboom's face. "Take that, old man!" The light strobed on and off several times.

Uncle Hoogaboom dropped his hand and staggered backwards into Hector and Wiliken.

"And now you two!" Slear quickly turned his flashing camera on the startled twins.

"Ka-poof him, Beezel! I can't see a thing! He's blinded me!" wailed Mimi.

"I can't see either!" All Beezel could see was a bright white light pulsing on and off. The light had driven the five magic words temporarily out of her head. The only thought in her head now was to turn off that darn light. Beezel heard a car engine start and the squeal of tyres as the black car pulled away from them.

Beezel heard Slear yell, "This is way bigger than you, Riebeeck! When I break this story, it's gonna be huge!"

After a few minutes, they could all see properly again.

"This is terrible," Beezel said. "Slear knows about

the magic of the Shrinking Coin *and* the Changing Coin!"

"I'm so sorry," said Wiliken. "If it weren't for me, Slear wouldn't even be here."

"Oh, I wouldn't worry too much about that," Uncle Hoogaboom said. "It's just his word against ours. He really can't prove anything without our cooperation now, can he?"

"Well, no." Beezel knew he was right, but still, she had a tennis ball of worry in the pit of her stomach. But Uncle Hoogaboom didn't seem to share her concern at all. He seemed downright jolly.

"The Changing Coin," Uncle Hoogaboom said as he gathered the girls on each side of him and gave them a squeeze. "I never thought I'd live to see its magic again. I've not seen that since Simon and I worked together."

Beezel's jaw dropped. "You *knew* Simon Serafin?"

Uncle Hoogaboom nodded. "When we were young men, about Wiliken's age, he came to work in the same circus I was working in. The Circus Oosterbeck, here in the Netherlands. He was the strong man, and I was the dog trainer and roustabout. We became fast friends. My father had given me the Shrinking Coin. I found out that his mother, the lead acrobat of the Romanian Circus Lumanararu, had given him the Changing Coin." He laughed. "As you can well imagine, we had quite a lot of fun."

"Shrinking and changing things together," Mimi said wistfully. "I wish I could have been there."

There was something bothering Beezel. Something was whirling about in the back of her head. Then she had it. She faced Uncle Hoogaboom. "David Copperfield's eyelashes!" Beezel said. "*That's* why you and Wiliken's grandpa couldn't find the treasure for all those years. It's a *shrunken* treasure!"

Uncle Hoogaboom grinned shyly and tugged on his beard. "Yes, since I was a boy, I've dreamed I would be the one who got to unshrink the treasure from that old galleon."

"That's the part I didn't mention to you guys the other night," Wiliken said. "Hoogaboom wanted to get together with Hector and me privately and tell him about the Shrinking Coin."

"But now," Uncle Hoogaboom said with enthusiasm, "there's no need for that! I can let these girls hear all about it. After all, they have a magic coin, too!"

Uncle Hoogaboom looked like he was about to launch into an explanation, but Hector stopped him. "Excuse me, Uncle," Hector said, motioning to the clam in Mimi's hands. "Maybe Mimi should un-ka-poof that dog and let it go back home now. And then I think we should take this conversation back to Wiliken's house and talk privately." He glanced around him. "Now's a good time, duck," he said to Mimi.

"Okay, little doggie," Mimi said. She put the clam down and pointed to it. Ka-poof. A confused but friendly dog wagged his tail at them.

Beezel watched as Mimi and Hector escorted the dog back across the darkening street. So there really was a Shrinking Coin. And Uncle Hoogaboom had known Simon! And somewhere, inside Pieter Riebeeck's house, was the entire treasure of a Spanish galleon. Knowing what she did now, she wanted to go on their treasure hunt, too.

CHaPTER TWELVE

as they walked the last couple of blocks to Wiliken's house, Uncle Hoogaboom hummed happily.

"We've heard there is a Mind-Reading Coin, too," Mimi said to him. "But we don't have any idea who has that one."

Wiliken let out a long whistle. "You could get into trouble with that one, I bet."

"I was always told," Uncle Hoogaboom said, "that the three coins had travelled the world several times together, and finally came to a Gypsy family in Romania several hundred years ago. They were a group of touring performers, much like your travelling circus, girls, but I'm sure not nearly as grand. One of those long-ago Gypsies married a long-ago Hoogaboom and gave my family the Shrinking

Coin." He stopped and tilted his head to one side in thought. "Someone from that Gypsy troupe might have given one of Simon's ancestors the Changing Coin. His mother was Romanian. I've never heard anything about where the Mind-Reading Coin is now."

Uncle Hoogaboom looked at Hector. "And nephew, you've known the girls had the Changing Coin?"

"Yes." Hector grinned. "But I was sworn to secrecy, Uncle."

They soon came to Wiliken's house and entered through Uncle Hoogaboom's shop.

Wiliken opened the door to the hallway. "Let's go up to my grandpa's apartment," he said. "I think he'd love for us to be there when we sort this all out." He grinned at Beezel and she felt her knees go a bit wobbly.

"Come on, Uncle Hoogaboom," Mimi said, grabbing his arm. "I want to know all about the Shrinking Coin."

They trudged up the steep stairway to the next floor.

"Here we are." Wiliken opened the door at the top of the landing, reached inside and flipped on a light.

"It's beautiful," Beezel managed to say as they walked in. Wiliken smiled at her. She sure hoped her cheeks weren't going to turn that awful bright red colour they sometimes did.

"It *is* nice, isn't it?" He waved them into a small but elegant sitting room. "Grandpa had good taste, didn't he, Hoogaboom?"

The old man nodded and closed the door behind him. "We'll need some privacy," Uncle Hoogaboom said.

The sitting room was paneled in dark wood. Paintings of ships hung on the walls in gold frames.

Across the room on the far wall was a brick fireplace. On each side was a brown leather sofa. Between them was a walnut coffee table. Nestled around the room were tables loaded to the edges with antiques.

"Let's sit over there," Wil said, pointing to the sofas. "We can get caught up on all this magic coin business. I want to hear about the Changing Coin."

Beezel sat next to Hector and Mimi on one sofa, and Uncle Hoogaboom and Wiliken sat on the other. Beezel explained how the Changing Coin worked to Wiliken and Uncle Hoogaboom. How you thought the five magic words, pointed at the person or animal you wanted to change and imagined a different animal.

"Ka-poof!" she said. "They will become that animal until I think the words in reverse order and point at them again. Then they'll change back into their original form. It works exactly the same way for Mimi. The Changing Coin is used to pass the magic down to someone else, but we don't have to have it with us to use its power. And because we're twins, we get to share the magic of the coin."

"We have to stay near each other, though," Mimi said, "or the magic doesn't work properly. And you can never, ever say the words out loud or write them down, or the magic will die for ever."

"So it's true that twins can share the magic of the coins. *Asjemenou!*" Uncle Hoogaboom exclaimed.

Hector interrupted him to translate for the twins. "He's not cursing—that just means 'Well, I'll be!'"

"That's the way mine works," Uncle Hoogaboom said, "with a few minor differences. As you saw with Mr Slear and his car, the Shrinking Coin can shrink objects *and* people—although I can't shrink myself, or for that matter, the coin itself. But it works in much the same way as the Changing Coin does for you girls. I think the five magic words, think of what I want to shrink and point to it. Then, zuuft! The object or person shrinks to one twelfth of its original size. If someone is six feet tall, they become six inches tall. If it is an object with things inside it, like a box of tools, everything inside the box shrinks proportionally."

"But why the number twelve?" Beezel asked.

"I'm not sure," Hoogaboom said. "It has always been a magical number. I imagine the real reason has been lost for ever."

"Wow!" Mimi said. "That would be so much fun. Does that mean you can keep shrinking someone down to the size of a flea?"

"That's right," Hoogaboom said. "But you can't shrink something so small you can no longer see it. No smaller than about the size of a pinhead."

Beezel hit her forehead with her hand. "Of course! That's how you've been making all the details for your models!"

"Guilty," Hoogaboom said, smiling. "But I didn't shrink the houses themselves. I made the models to fit the scale of my 'details.'"

"Why didn't you just shrink some real houses?"

Hector asked. "It would be easier than building them." He rubbed his chin. "Although I guess you'd get into some pretty big trouble if you shrank something like Notre Dame cathedral."

"Yes," Hoogaboom agreed. "I don't think the French would be too happy with me."

"But *could* you if you wanted to?" Beezel asked.

"No," Hoogaboom said. "When you want to shrink something, or someone, imagine you are standing in the middle of a 'shrinking circle.' You can shrink anything that falls within a hundred arms' lengths from the centre of your circle. The circle radiates out from where you stand. That's about three hundred feet."

"So you can't stand somewhere and point to a faraway house on a mountain and shrink it," Beezel said.

"That's right," Hoogaboom said. "And you can't shrink anything that is wider than one hundred arms' lengths as well. So you *can* stand a few feet away from a country cottage and shrink it, but you can't shrink a large building like a museum." He glanced at the twins. "The other rules are the same. When I want to unshrink someone or something, I think the words in reverse order, point and zuuft so the person or thing will return to its original size."

Uncle Hoogaboom stood up, walked over to where Hector was sitting and put his hand on his shoulder. "Nephew, you know I have no children of my own. You are my next of kin. So just as soon as Wiliken and I find the shrunken treasure, the Shrinking Coin is going to be yours. It is your legacy."

"Mine?" Hector stared up at his uncle, a shocked look on his face. "Are you sure?"

"Wow! That's great!" Mimi said as she patted a stunned Hector on the back. "You can be in our magic act!"

"This is why I wanted you to come to Amsterdam, Hector," Uncle Hoogaboom said. "The Shrinking Coin and its magic is the gift I told you I had for you. I knew I had to tell you what it was in person, to *show* you its magic for you to believe me. I had been waiting for a private moment with you and Wiliken." Uncle Hoogaboom smiled at the girls. "But now I know these two have their own magic coin, and from my old friend Simon as well! So we can talk about this out in the open among us!"

He looked at Beezel, raised one eyebrow and smiled at her. "And I bet right now, you are wondering why Wiliken already knew about my coin, and why I wanted him to be with me when I told Hector, aren't you?"

Beezel smiled back. "Well, yes."

"Then I will tell you." Uncle Hoogaboom sat back down on the sofa across from them and leaned forwards. "You see, the Hoogabooms and the Riebeecks have known each other for a very long time. We Hoogabooms have always been an argumentative lot, and it caused problems when the time came to pass down the magic. Who was most worthy? The eldest child? The smartest? The most honorable?

"Even after an heir was chosen, the remaining Hoogabooms managed to bicker over the coin itself. Once a distant relative of mine even stole the coin from his own sister and tried to hold it hostage for the magic. Luckily, it was returned to her, and she kept the magic, but after that incident, my ancestors decided something had to be done.

"So, the Hoogabooms charged the Riebeecks with the safekeeping of the Shrinking Coin. At the appropriate time, as each generation of Hoogabooms agreed on the next heir, and before they had time to argue over it, the Riebeecks would bring the coin out of its hiding place for the transfer of the magic."

Uncle Hoogaboom stroked his chin. "Having the coin safely hidden away allowed us to use the magic without coming to blows every other day. After all, we didn't have to have the coin in our possession to use its powers!" He smiled at the twins.

"And we Riebeecks," Wiliken said, "would get certain things in return. After all, knowing someone who could zuuft things came in very handy, especially for a shipping company. There has been a lot of shrunken cargo aboard my family's ships over the years."

"After the magic was passed down," Uncle Hoogaboom said, "one Riebeeck would be shrunk by the newly empowered Hoogaboom. This tiny Riebeeck would be taken by the other Riebeecks to help hide the Shrinking Coin until the next transfer of the coin's power." He chuckled. "Of course, he was always unshrunk afterwards."

They were quiet a minute. Beezel imagined everyone was lost in their own thoughts of the magic coins and their powers. Hector broke the silence.

"So, Uncle," Hector said, "what you're telling me is that not only has our family had the Shrinking Coin for a very long time, but that somehow, one of our relatives helped hide a shrunken treasure in the Riebeecks' house?"

Uncle Hoogaboom and Wiliken exchanged looks, and Wiliken smiled. "Something like that," Uncle Hoogaboom said.

"Uncle Hoogaboom, I've been thinking," Beezel said. "How did you get the treasure in the first place?"

Uncle Hoogaboom started to answer her when there was a loud knock at the sitting room door. Wiliken got up to answer it.

An older dark-haired man entered the room.

"Ah, Edwin," Uncle Hoogaboom said with a hint of distaste in his voice.

Beezel recognised the man from the shop on the day they had arrived. She studied his face. *What an odd-looking person*, she thought to herself. He seemed to be the combination of two animals. He had the eyes of a deer: big, wide and brown. *But his mouth* . . . He gnawed on the edge of his bottom lip. She supposed it was a nervous habit, like Mimi's twirling of her hair. *Still, it makes him seem like a mouse . . . or a rat*, she thought.

"My apologies," Edwin said stiffly. "I did not know you had company, Wiliken." He shot Hector and the twins a quick look.

Wiliken introduced them to Edwin. He politely nodded at each of them in turn.

"Since I am leaving in a few days, I came to get my clock," Edwin said, gesturing towards the mantel. "I was pleased that my cousin left it to me in his will. I must say, it came as a surprise that he didn't leave it to you, Wiliken, along with everything else."

The bitter edge to his voice caused Beezel and Mimi to exchange glances.

"Take the clock, Edwin," Wiliken said. "Grandpa wanted you to have it."

Edwin hurried over to the mantel and grabbed the clock. He nodded briskly at Uncle Hoogaboom and left the sitting room. Before he left, he turned and muttered something to Wiliken in Dutch.

"What did he say?" Mimi asked Hector.

"I'm not sure," Hector said to the twins. "But I think he said that Wiliken should live the rest of his years as a donkey." He shrugged. "Either that or he said he looked like a baboon. I'm still a little slow on the translating."

"It was the baboon, nephew," Uncle Hoogaboom confirmed.

Wiliken snorted. "This is from a guy who spills his guts to Slear about our family?" He eyed the doorway to the hall. "And he calls *me* a baboon?"

Uncle Hoogaboom had grown quiet. "I've never liked that man," he said. "And there are very few people I can say that about." He took a deep breath and glanced at his watch. Then it was as if he had forgotten all about Edwin *and* telling them about the treasure.

"Look at the time! It's almost nine. Well, now, I think I'm going to call it a day." He tapped his watch with one finger. "I am an old man, after all, and need my rest."

He waved a finger in the air. "I have an excellent idea. Hector, after you and the girls have been to the flea market tomorrow, come by the house. Wiliken will join us, and we'll have dinner and finish talking." He smiled mischievously. "Besides, I have a surprise to show you!"

"Surprise?" Hector started, but Uncle Hooga-boom was already headed for the door.

He nodded firmly to Hector as he rushed by him.

"So, it's decided then. I will see you all sometime in the afternoon."

They stood staring at one another, speechless. Then Uncle Hoogaboom popped his head back inside the doorway. "And don't worry about Mr Slear—he has no proof of anything. I've seen his kind come and go before. Just ignore him. Sleep well."

That night as Beezel lay in bed at the Merlin Hotel, she went over everything Wiliken and Uncle Hoogaboom had told them about the Shrinking Coin and their families' unusual friendship. She tried to fall asleep, but one person's face kept sneaking back into her mind. It was Edwin. As she finally nodded off, she dreamed he was a giant rat nibbling at Wiliken's front door.

"Just *what* do you think you are doing?" she demanded of the Edwin in her dream.

"I'm going to find the treasure," he said as he bit off a chunk of the door and proceeded to eat it.

CHAPTER THIRTEEN

What about this one?" Mimi said as she held up a shirt in front of her sister.

"It doesn't really matter, does it?" Beezel said. It was late Monday morning and they were going to go to the Noordermarkt flea market with Hector. Beezel felt like she had been ready for days.

She and Mimi had already taken Gumdrop the dog for an early walk. They had played catch with her back in the room, although Gumdrop refused to release the ball of socks they tossed her. She just kept squeezing it in her jaws.

"Of course it matters," Mimi said as she threw the shirt down on the floor and pulled another one off a hanger in the closet. "We're going to see Wil later."

"Wiliken," Beezel corrected.

"*Wil*," Mimi insisted. "When we go over to Uncle

Hoogaboom's house after the flea market, I want to look nice." She eyed her sister. "And you should, too, Beezel. Get up and brush your hair. You look like you were dropped in a blender."

"Gee, thanks."

Mimi giggled. "Well, don't get grumpy about it."

Beezel combed out her hair, rebraided it and slipped on her sneakers. Mimi was still standing in the centre of a mound of clothes.

"I can't make up my mind," Mimi said.

"Just put something on." Beezel plucked a blue shirt from off the floor. "Here, this looks good on you."

Mimi's face lit up. "It does?" She slipped on the shirt and her jeans. "Thanks, Beez."

Beezel smiled at her sister. "No problem."

Hector and the girls caught a tram that took them near Uncle Hoogaboom's house and walked the rest of the way to the Noordermarkt.

The flea market was bustling with activity. Beezel couldn't believe all the different things that were for sale: fabric, clothes, jewellery, furniture and knick-knacks. The threesome spent the rest of the after-noon buying souvenirs for their family and friends in the Trimoni Circus. Beezel even found a sequined headdress for Meredith the clairvoyant to wear while she told fortunes.

Before they headed back down the Prinsengracht to Uncle Hoogaboom's house, they wandered around inside a bookstore they discovered on the corner. Mimi went directly to the art book section. Hector found an English newspaper and a chair to read it in, and Beezel got lost in a book of photographs of the Dutch countryside.

After some time, Beezel looked out the store window and realised that the afternoon had slipped by. The flea market had packed up and gone home, and the sunlight had begun to turn the rosy shade of early evening.

She pulled Mimi away from the art books and woke Hector from where he had fallen asleep with a newspaper over his face. After buying some postcards to take home, they left to walk to Uncle Hoogaboom's house.

"I can't wait until I'm a famous artist and get to live in a place like Amsterdam!" Mimi said.

"It's a big world with lots to see," Hector said as he smiled at the twins. "Whichever direction you each decide to take, I hope you get to see it all."

Beezel almost stopped walking when she heard

that, but caught herself in time. Mimi had talked about being an artist ever since she could remember. And Beezel wanted to travel and see the world. But she had never really thought about what it meant before now. When she and Mimi grew up, they wouldn't still be the Trimoni Twins, performing magic in their little circus. She walked quietly, chewing on this thought, and didn't say a word the rest of the way to Uncle Hoogaboom's shop.

Mimi opened the red door and waved hello to Gaidic, who was busy helping a customer.

"I think Wiliken is upstairs," she called to the girls with a smile.

"Let's go get him," Mimi said to Beezel. The twins left Hector in the detail room while they went up the stairs to Wiliken's apartment.

"Wil!" Mimi called as she knocked on the door. "It's us!"

Wiliken opened the door and smiled at them. Beezel felt her heart flutter and quickly glanced down at her shoes.

"Well, hello, you two," he said.

"Are you coming to Uncle Hoogaboom's for dinner?" Mimi asked him.

"You bet," Wiliken said.

"Are we too early?" Beezel asked him.

"Nah," he said. "Hoogaboom wouldn't mind us helping him cook. Just let me find my shoes."

The phone in the sitting room rang and Wiliken answered it. "Hallo?" he said. "Oh, hi, Stephen!" He covered the mouthpiece and said, "I'm going to take this in the den. It's my agent. Can you hang up when I get in there?" He started for the hall and stopped. "Make yourselves at home. Or you can go on down to Hoogaboom's. I won't be too long. He probably just wants to nag me about something I haven't done." He grinned. "Maybe you guys could turn him into something for me?"

Beezel held the phone and hung up when she heard Wiliken pick up. "What should we do?" she asked her sister. "Do you want to go downstairs?"

"Not right now." Mimi reached inside her backpack and took out Gumdrop's plastic container.

"Oh, no, no, no," Beezel said. "Please tell me that isn't Gumdrop."

"Of course it is. I went back down and got her before we left. After all, I didn't see her *all day* yesterday while we were sightseeing," Mimi said. "I couldn't leave her alone today, too."

"Mimi," Beezel said as she watched her sister

open the container and pour Gumdrop the ladybird on to her lap. "Don't do it . . . You know what Hector said."

Ka-poof. Gumdrop was a small golden hamster. She nibbled at Mimi's fingertips.

"There," said Mimi. "She can run around on my lap until Wiliken gets back. Then I'll ka-poof her back into a ladybird."

Beezel marvelled at Mimi's devotion to her pet. Anyone else would have left the snake at home and brought it back a souvenir at best. "Just keep an eye on her."

Mimi let Gumdrop run up and down her sleeve. "What do you think Uncle Hoogaboom's surprise is tonight?" she asked Beezel.

"I don't know," Beezel said. "He's acting very mysterious about it, isn't he?" She thought for a minute. "But I hope it's that we get to help search for the treasure, don't you?"

"Yes!" Mimi said as she scratched the hamster's ears. "Oh, I know! We could form two teams. You, Uncle Hoogaboom and Hector could be on one team. Wil and I could be on the other." She nodded happily. "We'd find the treasure faster that way."

"Why should *you* get to have Wiliken on *your*

114

team?" Beezel asked. She felt her cheeks getting hot. "I'd like to have him on my team, too."

"Oh." Mimi narrowed her eyes at Beezel. "So you *like* Wil, do you? Well, I like him, too." She nodded, sending her hair bouncing. "Besides, I saw him *first*."

"You did not!"

"Well, I *recognised* him first!" Mimi said.

"What?" Beezel couldn't believe her ears. "Just because you *recognise* someone first doesn't mean you *own* them!"

"Well, I like him *more* than you do," Mimi said as she stood up. "Why do you always have to like the same things I do anyway?"

"*What?*" Beezel said again, standing in front of Mimi. "I don't like *any* of the same things you do. You like art, and . . . and . . . *reptiles*! I just *happen* to like Wiliken, too!" She gasped and covered her mouth. She had actually said it out loud.

Mimi's mouth dropped open. "Beezel Marie Trimoni! You have a crush on a boy!" she said disbelievingly. "You've *never* had a crush on a boy before!"

"Well," Beezel said, blushing, "I've never met a boy like Wiliken before."

"Well . . ." Mimi crossed her arms. "He's much too old for you."

"Well, then," Beezel said, putting her hands on her hips, "he's too old for you, too!"

The twins stood quietly facing each other. Beezel coughed and cleared her throat. She guessed this was what was meant by "an awkward moment."

"Listen," Beezel finally said. "I don't think he'd be interested in either one of us. We're only eleven, and he's seventeen."

Mimi nodded at her sadly.

"Let's go down to Uncle Hoogaboom's shop and wait," Beezel said. "I want to see his details again now that I know he shrank them." She was trying hard not to let the anger she felt towards Mimi a moment ago creep back into her voice.

"Okay," Mimi said. "Just let me put Gum-drop . . ." Her eyes widened. Mimi patted her sleeves and checked her pants legs. "Oh, no! Gumdrop fell off my lap when I stood up to yell at you!"

The girls crawled on the carpet and called for the little snake-turned-hamster. Beezel saw something golden brown scoot along the wall and behind a piano.

"Over here, Mimi!" Beezel said. She grabbed the side of the piano and pulled it away from the wall a few inches.

"There you are!" Mimi said to Gumdrop the hamster. "Come out of there, sweetie!"

But Gumdrop wasn't interested in coming out from behind the piano. She had found a hole in the wall. Gumdrop gave two quick sniffs at the entrance and then quickly disappeared inside it.

"Oh, no! We'll never get her out of there!" Mimi burst into tears. "She's gone for ever this time, Beezel!"

Beezel stared at her twin. "I've got an idea."

Mimi wiped her eyes on her sleeve. "What?" she sobbed.

"Ka-poof me and I'll go after her. But do it right now—she could get lost inside the walls."

"But what will I change you into?" Mimi asked.

Beezel examined the hole in the wall. "A ferret," she said. "I'll be big enough to carry Gumdrop back out once I find her and still fit through the hole. Hurry up!"

Ka-poof. Beezel was a grey ferret. She squeezed through the hole and found herself sitting on top of a large drainpipe. She sniffed the air, and for some reason, known only to the small part of her brain that temporarily functioned in a ferretlike manner, turned left and began to run along its length.

Beezel kept a sharp eye out for the brown hamster. As she scurried along inside the wall, she passed a few dead beetles, a mouse nest and a broken glass bottle. She stopped and sniffed again. There was fresh air ahead. Her ears twitched and Beezel heard something. Something alive.

She looked down the pipe. An intersecting wall created a dead end ahead. Cut into the wall a few inches above the pipe was an air vent. Daylight streamed in through its horizontal slats, creating stripes of light. Next to the air vent, in the middle of one stripe, Beezel saw Gumdrop.

Gumdrop, standing on her hind legs, seemed completely preoccupied by a spider that had built a web from a wooden beam down to the top of the air vent.

Beezel hurried next to Gumdrop and was contemplating the best approach to grabbing her when she heard voices outside. She peered out the air vent through the spiderwebs and into the small rear garden of Wiliken's house.

Below her, she saw Edwin and Slear talking.

Beezel forgot all about her mission to save Gumdrop and listened carefully.

"You're sure they're not going to come out here?" Slear asked Edwin.

"I assure you, they are far too obsessed with their little treasure hunt indoors to even peek out the windows," Edwin said. "Look at the state of things out here. Does it look like anyone comes outside?"

Slear glanced around the overgrown garden. "I see your point." He put his hand on Edwin's shoulder. "Listen, I believe you now about this Shrinking Coin stuff. When you first tried to sell me that story, I thought you were nuts. You know, like you wanted to sell me an 'Elvis is an alien' kinda thing.

"But I saw it myself, and I'm telling you, that hocus-pocus is amazing. They wiggle their fingers at you and . . . Zam! Pow! Things start to happen. It's not just the old man, it's those girls, too. I've seen cars shrink, people shrink . . . dogs turn into rocks."

A clam, you jerk, Beezel thought. *It was a clam!*

"We've got to get our hands on that stuff, pal," Slear said. "This is way better than any dirt we can dig up on star boy. Bigger even than that treasure you're knocking yourself out looking for."

Edwin was quiet, gazing at a potted tree in the corner of the garden. "I've been thinking," he said finally. "We should formalise our relationship. So there are no misunderstandings about the division of payment."

"Now you're speaking my language!" Slear thumped Edwin on the back. "The green stuff, right? Am I right?"

"I cannot possibly see how we are speaking the *same* language," Edwin said huffily. "But if what you are saying is that I'm seeking adequate payment for my information, then yes."

"Edwin, old chum," Slear said, spreading his hands wide, "name your price. If you go in on this with me, we won't be rich, we'll be *filthy* rich."

"I think fifty percent of everything you make from the Shrinking Coin, or the stories about Wiliken, or anything related to either of those, sounds fair to me, don't you?" Edwin handed Slear a paper. "I had this drawn up, just to make sure we understand each other."

"Lawyers, eh?" Slear snatched the paper from Edwin. "Whatever floats your boat, Edwin." Beezel saw him scribble something on the paper. "Now spill it. You said you had something else for me."

Edwin looked left and right. "There is a coin they *must* have to give the shrinking magic to anyone else. I have no idea where it is, but knowing my family the way I do, it is inside this house somewhere."

"So we're looking for a coin. Roger that. Two coins, I guess if those twins have their own, right?" Slear said.

Edwin nodded. "I would imagine so."

"Listen," Slear said. "We're guaranteed a Pulitzer Prize with this stuff. It will simply blow every other news story off the charts." He leaned over and patted Edwin's shoulder. "You'll be in the history books, pal."

Edwin appeared amused. "That could be enter-taining, yes. But that's not my particular interest."

"Oh, that's right, you're more of a gold and silver man, aren't you?" Slear snorted. "You've made some progress on that treasure hunt yourself, am I right?"

"Yes," Edwin said. "I think I have a pretty good idea where it is. Once I find it, if we can somehow manage to get that idiot Hoogaboom to unshrink it, it will be quite an inheritance."

"Then let's get to work," Slear said happily.

"Oh, one more thing," Edwin said coolly. "The

papers you've signed? They say I get eighty percent of the Spanish treasure."

"Well, of course you do!" Slear slapped Edwin on the back again. "Let's go have a drink and work out the details, whaddya say?" He tilted back his head and laughed. "This is going to be something," he said. "We're going to prove to the world that magic really does exist!"

They began to walk towards the house.

"You know, buddy," Slear said to Edwin. "If you think about it, a shrunken treasure chest, loaded with all that miniature loot, would be spectacular. I wonder how little it is. Maybe we could open it on TV! Live coverage! We could get some scientists on to verify a few things . . ."

Slear's voice drifted off as he disappeared from Beezel's view.

Beezel pulled her head away from the vent. Her little ferret heart was beating like a drum. She turned her head. Luckily, Gumdrop was still mesmerised by the spider building its web.

Beezel opened her mouth and snatched a surprised Gumdrop by the scruff of her neck. Then she ran as fast as she could down the pipe back to the hole in the sitting room wall.

When Mimi saw Beezel run out of the hole carrying a wriggling Gumdrop in her mouth, she quickly took Gumdrop from her and un-ka-poofed her sister. She hugged Beezel with one arm and said, "Thank you so much!" while she carefully held the little hamster in her other hand.

Mimi ka-poofed Gumdrop back into a ladybird and put her inside her container. "I'm not going to lose you again!" she scolded her. She put Gumdrop in her backpack and slipped it on. "And I'm not taking this backpack off until we get back to our room!"

When Gumdrop was safe and sound again, Beezel told Mimi about the conversation she had heard in the garden between Slear and Edwin.

"Mimi," Beezel said, "Edwin knows about the treasure. He thinks he knows where it is. And he told Slear about the Shrinking Coin. But the worst thing is, Slear wants to sell the story of the magic coins. He wants to be famous for discovering *real* magic!"

"Oh my gosh!" Mimi said as she put her hand to her mouth. "We have to tell someone!"

Beezel agreed. The twins ran down the hall and peeked into the den. They saw Wiliken deep in conversation on the phone. "Let's go find Hector and Uncle Hoogaboom," Beezel said.

The twins left Wiliken's apartment and ran down the flight of stairs to Uncle Hoogaboom's shop. Hector was helping Gaidic organise a pile of miniature living room furniture for a display in the shop window.

"Uh, Hector," Mimi said, "we need to talk to you about something."

"And we need Uncle Hoogaboom," Beezel said.

"Oh, he's on the third floor," Gaidic said. "He and Pieter converted the attic into a studio some years ago. Go on up. But knock loudly or he won't hear you." She shrugged. "He won't let anyone in there. The only other person who ever got to go inside was Pieter." She stared up at the ceiling as if she could see through Wiliken's apartment straight up to Uncle Hoogaboom in the attic. "I hope he's all right up there," she said, with a note of concern in her voice. "See if he wants some tea, will you?"

"Come on, Hector," Mimi said as she pulled Hector away from Gaidic.

"Easy on the shirt, chickadee," Hector said. "I'm coming!"

The twins, followed by Hector, rushed up the

stairs to the landing on the third floor. On the way, Hector tried to get an explanation, but the girls assured him they would tell him everything once they were with Uncle Hoogaboom.

Hector tried to open the door to the studio, but it was locked. He knocked loudly on the door, and after a minute or two, Uncle Hoogaboom appeared, carrying a tube of green paint in one hand and a tiny paintbrush in the other.

"Well, hallo!" he greeted them as he stepped out of his studio and closed the door behind him. He stuffed the articles he was carrying into his already bulging front pockets and glanced at his watch. "Is it time for dinner already?"

Beezel and Mimi quickly told Uncle Hoogaboom all about Beezel's adventure inside the wall and the conversation she'd overheard while she was saving Gumdrop.

Uncle Hoogaboom listened intently, occasionally scratching his beard with one hand. By the time the girls were finished, it was clear Uncle Hoogaboom was quite upset.

He paced across the landing, muttering to himself in Dutch.

"What's he saying, Hector?" Beezel whispered.

"Either that he wants to boil Edwin in oil," Hector said, "or he wants fried fish for dinner."

"The first one!" Uncle Hoogaboom announced as he locked the door to his studio and put the key in his pocket. "Come with me—we need to talk to Wiliken."

They hurried down one flight and knocked on Wiliken's door.

"Hi!" Wiliken said cheerily as he surveyed the group standing on his landing. "I'm sorry about that phone call," he said to Beezel and Mimi. "When an agent calls, you have to answer. Otherwise, you might miss out on a role you want."

"Oh, are you going to be in another movie?" Mimi gushed, stepping in front of Beezel.

"Yep!" Wiliken said. "I just got offered a part in the remake of *The Three Musketeers.*"

Mimi squealed. "Oh my gosh!"

"So come inside, and let's celebrate!" Wiliken said, waving them in.

Beezel felt terrible. Wiliken was so happy, and now they were going to ruin it with her news.

"Wiliken, son," Uncle Hoogaboom said. "Have a seat—we need to talk."

When Uncle Hoogaboom finished telling him

what Beezel had heard, Wiliken stood up and said, "The Amsterdam Riebeecks have always known about the Shrinking Coin, and kept that knowledge close to home. I don't know how Edwin found out about it. Maybe he overheard my grandpa talking. But Edwin is now the first Riebeeck to ever break the trust we've had with your family, Hoogaboom." Wiliken's jaw clenched as he looked at him. "Edwin came home a few minutes ago and went back to his room. Would you come down there with me in case I need a translator?"

"It would be my pleasure," Uncle Hoogaboom said.

"What are you going to do?" Mimi asked.

"I'm going to throw Edwin and his things out of my grandfather's house," Wiliken said as he turned and sauntered down the hall.

"You know what?" Mimi whispered to Beezel as she clasped her hands under her chin. "Just now, he looked *exactly* like he did in *Half Past Midnight.*" She sighed. "He's *so* cute."

"He really is," Beezel agreed. "Definitely."

The girls sat on the sofa with Hector and listened to the heated conversation going on down the hall. Beezel and Mimi heard Edwin and Uncle

Hoogaboom yelling. Once they heard Wiliken blurt out, "Yeah? Well, at least I didn't sell out my family for a few measly bucks!"

It grew quiet, and after several minutes, they heard someone stomping down the hallway towards them. Edwin stormed past carrying two suitcases, followed closely by Uncle Hoogaboom and Wiliken. Edwin set one suitcase down and opened the door to the stairwell. Looking over his shoulder, he picked up his bag, shouted something, marched out and kicked the door shut behind him.

Everyone turned to Uncle Hoogaboom. His face was grim.

"What did he say that time?" Beezel asked him.

"That Wiliken will be very sorry for doing this." Uncle Hoogaboom patted Wiliken on the back and sighed. "This is serious. Edwin believes he knows where the treasure has been hidden in our house. We can keep him out until we find it, Wiliken, but the fact that Edwin has also confirmed to Mr Slear that the shrinking magic is real is a dangerous combination. And he suspects the girls have magic as well. I imagine that Mr Slear will be spending a lot of his free time watching us."

Wiliken looked at the closed door and nodded in

agreement. "You're right. Slear will put us under a microscope just as soon as he can. You won't be able to open the refrigerator door without seeing him looking back at you."

Beezel shivered. The idea of Slear's face greeting her at every turn was enough to give her nightmares.

"Given what has happened," Uncle Hoogaboom said, tugging thoughtfully on his beard, "I think the best thing would be to transfer the magic to Hector now. Afterwards, I'll just continue to act as if nothing has changed here. For all Slear will know, I'll still have the magic myself." He looked at the girls. "And you will have to be very careful. Perhaps you should refrain from using the magic, except when you are performing on stage, just for a while, until this blows over. He could be watching you, after all."

"But Uncle Hoogaboom," Mimi said, "what if Slear just keeps pestering all of us?"

"Then we'll have to meet with him and persuade him to stop," Hector said, his arms crossed over his chest. "I think a few good ka-poofs and a couple of zuufts ought to do it, don't you, Uncle?"

Uncle Hoogaboom nodded. "I can only speak

129

for zuufting, but it's usually a very convincing argument."

"Just promise you'll let me come with you." Wiliken grinned. "That guy has driven me crazy for months."

"Then it is decided. That is what we will do." Uncle Hoogaboom nodded with satisfaction. "It's time to give Hector the magic."

CHAPTER FOURTEEN

But what about Gaidic?" Wiliken said. "She's still downstairs."

"You're quite right," Uncle Hoogaboom said. "We can't have her in the house. Not with the practising and all."

"You could just send her home a little early," Wiliken said. "She won't mind. Close up the shop."

"Yes," Uncle Hoogaboom said. "That's just what I'll do."

"Excuse me, Uncle," Hector said. "What practising?"

"You'll need to practise shrinking things around the house." Uncle Hoogaboom nodded decisively. "You can't stroll around the city with that kind of magic in your fingertips without practising first."

"Are you *sure* you want to give it to me right

now?" Hector seemed less than pleased. "I thought you wanted to find the treasure first," he protested. "You wanted to be the one to unshrink it. You told us that."

Uncle Hoogaboom shook his head. "That was my dream for many years. Pieter's and mine. But more important is keeping the Shrinking Coin and the Changing Coin a secret from the world. It's what we've always done." He shook his head. "I swear it! No one is going to prove there is shrinking magic on my shift!"

"That's the spirit, Hoogaboom!" Wiliken said as he opened the apartment door and started down the stairs. "Let's send Gaidic home and lock up!"

They trooped down the stairs to Hoogaboom's shop. Hector and the twins stood by the hall doorway as Uncle Hoogaboom did everything but shove poor Gaidic out the door.

As she said, *"Goedenacht!"* she glanced over at Hector with a definite "What is going on?" look on her face.

"Goodnight, Gaidic! See you tomorrow!" Wiliken called as Uncle Hoogaboom shut the door after her and locked it.

"Wiliken," Uncle Hoogaboom said, "may I have a

word with you alone, please?" Uncle Hoogaboom and Wiliken talked softly together in a corner of the detail room for a few minutes.

Beezel and Mimi turned to Hector and saw a stricken look on his face.

"What's wrong?" Beezel asked.

"Gaidic knew we were up to something," Hector said sadly. "I don't like her feeling left out. Or that we don't like her."

"Or that *you* don't like her," Mimi said as she patted his back.

Hector nodded and whispered, "And I'm not sure I *want* the Shrinking Coin. I've seen the trouble the Changing Coin has gotten you two into. What if I bungle the whole thing up? What if *I'm* the one who accidentally blurts out the five magic words and the magic is lost for ever?" He wiped his hands over his face. "See? I'm sweating just thinking about it."

"Don't worry," Beezel assured him. "You'll do a great job of protecting the coin. And we'll help you, won't we, Mimi?"

Mimi hugged Hector. "You bet. And don't forget, at home we're just in the next trailer over!"

"I apologise for excluding you," Uncle

Hoogaboom said as he and Wiliken walked over to them. "We've made a decision. Wiliken and I have something further to discuss with all of you before we transfer the shrinking magic to Hector."

They followed Uncle Hoogaboom into his apartment. He led them into a small front room. A comfy-looking blue sofa faced a small brick fireplace. Two overstuffed chairs covered in a red floral pattern were to one side. A coffee table, cluttered with some of Hoogaboom's details and several books, was in front of the sofa. In one corner was a large rolltop desk, looking every bit as stuffed as Uncle Hoogaboom's pockets. The whole room, Beezel thought, was very snug and welcoming.

Hector and the girls sat on the sofa. Uncle Hoogaboom and Wiliken each took a chair.

Beezel watched Wiliken from the sofa. He caught her gaze and winked at her. The effect on her was so strong, she was glad she was already sitting down.

Wiliken cleared his throat. "Hoogaboom and I were talking just now," he said. "And we have a favour to ask of you . . . after Hector gets the magic, of course." He nodded to Hector. "We think that what would be best all the way around is to find the treasure while you're still here. That way Hector could unshrink it, and Hoogaboom and I could have it stored safely in a bank, away from Edwin and Slear's greedy mitts."

"Oh my gosh, Beezel!" Mimi said as she grabbed her sister and hugged her. "We're finally going to get to go on that treasure hunt!"

"But," Beezel said, "how are we supposed to find it in just a few days when Uncle Hoogaboom's been looking for it for twenty-two years?"

"That's what we want to tell you," Wiliken said.

"You see, there are a few things you don't know," Uncle Hoogaboom said. "One of them is the answer to your question yesterday."

"About how you ended up with a shrunken treasure in the first place?" Beezel said.

Uncle Hoogaboom nodded. "And Pieter left us something we want to share with you as well. But it will make more sense when you understand where the treasure came from, so we will tell you that first.

"Almost four hundred years ago," Uncle Hoogaboom began, "the Riebeecks owned a heavily armed merchant ship. Koen Riebeeck was its captain. He was authorised by the Dutch government to raid the Spanish treasure fleets coming back from the New World. Engel Hoogaboom, a bit of a rogue and an adventurer, signed aboard one of his voyages.

"Koen Riebeeck captured a Spanish treasure galleon and brought it into Amsterdam's harbour. When it became clear that the government wasn't going to share the treasure as agreed, the two men put their heads together. They decided Engel Hoogaboom would shrink the treasure for safekeeping and Koen Riebeeck would hide the shrunken treasure inside his house."

Uncle Hoogaboom waved his hand around the room. "This very same house. And it was a good arrangement. Engel Hoogaboom knew that without him to unshrink the treasure, it was practically worthless. And Koen Riebeeck knew that without him, Hoogaboom would never know where the treasure was hidden."

"Very clever," Hector interrupted. "Good thinking on both their parts. It was like a fail-safe."

"What happened to the ship?" Beezel asked.

"After Koen Riebeeck hid the shrunken treasure," Wiliken said, "the two men sank the ship. But the Dutch government never really believed the treasure had gone down with the ship in the harbour. Days later, Koen Riebeeck fought the government troops that had come to take him prisoner and was killed."

"What happened to Engel Hoogaboom?" Hector asked.

"They imprisoned him," Uncle Hoogaboom said. "He lived long enough in prison to send for the Shrinking Coin. Koen Riebeeck's wife and Engel Hoogaboom's brother went to the prison to get the magic from him before he died. Eventually the coin made its way to me."

Beezel thought for a minute. "But since Koen Riebeeck died, and he was the only one who knew where he had hidden the treasure, isn't it lost for ever?"

"Oh, not for ever, certainly," Uncle Hoogaboom said as he winked at Wiliken. "We know it is in this house somewhere. We have their word on it, and we have something else."

Uncle Hoogaboom went to his desk and retrieved a large manila envelope. He handed it to Wiliken.

"This is something that my grandfather left me," Wiliken said.

"I had gone away on one of my buying trips," Uncle Hoogaboom said sadly. "I wish I had never gone. When I came back, I found out that Pieter had died."

"But before he died, he found the treasure," Wiliken said.

"He *found* it?" Hector said.

"Yes, but once he found it," Wiliken said, "he thought someone else was after it, so he put it in a new hiding place, just until Hoogaboom got back."

"After what you heard in the garden today, Beezel," Uncle Hoogaboom said, "I am certain Pieter was worried that Edwin was after the treasure for himself."

Wiliken undid the clasp on the envelope and pulled out a sheet of writing paper and a torn piece of old parchment. "This is the only thing we've had, for hundreds of years, that told us anything about the treasure." He held the parchment where they could see it. On it, in Dutch, were written several lines of text.

"I'll translate it for you," Uncle Hoogaboom said as he took the parchment from Wiliken.

> *Through walls like ice*
> *Past wood and metal*
> *Guarded by souls of sailors lost*
> *Lies the Spanish treasure*
> *Safe in Magda's capable hands*

138

"Who in the world is Magda?" Hector asked.

"Or *what* is she?" Uncle Hoogaboom said. "We have no idea."

"Hoogaboom and my grandpa have been trying all along to use that clue to find the treasure." Wiliken held up the other sheet of paper. "But this says my grandpa found it by accident. And right before he died, he wrote a note telling us where he hid it."

"So, you already know where it is?" A disappointed Mimi flopped back against the sofa. "Boy, that was the world's shortest treasure hunt."

"Wait a minute," Hector said. "Pieter told you exactly where it is, you've looked, and you *still* haven't found it? Boy, you *do* need help."

"Trust me," Wiliken said. "We've been looking for weeks, and we haven't found a thing."

"Where did he tell you he hid it?" Beezel asked.

"Let me read this to you," Wiliken said as he looked at the paper.

Wiliken—

 I found the treasure in a hollowed-out brick when the plumber came to fix a drainpipe in the kitchen, not three feet from where I fixed my morning tea all these years. Can you believe that?

I now suspect that someone else is after the treasure, so I have put it in my den for safekeeping.

I fear my days here on this earth are drawing to a close. I am sorry I did not know you better. I leave you with this bit of wisdom to remember me by: the greatest treasures are in the smallest pleasures.

Your Opa, Pieter Riebeeck

"Do you think someone stole it from the den?" Beezel said.

Wiliken shook his head. "I don't think so. No one knew about this letter except Hoogaboom and me. That's why we want you guys to help us. We need some fresh eyes in that room. We're hoping that while you are here, we can give the den one last scouring, sort of an 'all hands on deck' approach."

"Oh!" Mimi jumped up. "Can we go look now?"

Uncle Hoogaboom smiled at Mimi. "Of course. But if you don't mind," he said, "I want to get the magic transferred to Hector first. It's been weighing heavily on me since you girls told me about the conversation in the garden. Are you ready, Hector?"

Hector nodded slowly. "I'll do my best to protect it, Uncle."

Uncle Hoogaboom rifled through his pockets and brought out a silver key. He went back to his desk, unlocked the top drawer and took out a small gold box. He brought it over to where they were sitting and held it out for them to admire.

"It's a beautiful thing, isn't it?" Uncle Hoogaboom said to Wiliken. "Your grandfather left it in his will to me, to give to you when it was time to pass on the magic of the Shrinking Coin."

Beezel looked at the box. It was about eight inches long and four inches wide, gold, with a pattern of flowers engraved over its surface. Across the opening of the box, someone had pressed a wax seal.

"I know Pieter would have loved to give the Shrinking Coin to Hector according to our families' tradition . . ." Uncle Hoogaboom's voice caught and he cleared his throat. "But he would be so proud to know that you were here to do it for him." He handed the box to Wiliken. "Pieter's will didn't say what was in the box, but I'm sure it is the location of the Shrinking Coin."

Wiliken ran his finger over the seal. "Should I

open it now?" he asked. Uncle Hoogaboom nodded.

The twins leaned forwards as Wiliken broke the seal. He opened the box. It was empty.

CHAPTER FIFTEEN

I don't get it," Hector said. "Why would someone put a seal over an empty box?"

"Maybe they wanted you to know it was empty on purpose," Beezel said. "But that doesn't make much sense either."

Uncle Hoogaboom had been so upset at the sight of the empty box that Wiliken had made him sit down. Mimi brought him a glass of water from his kitchen.

"I don't understand," Uncle Hoogaboom said. "It was locked in that desk since Pieter's lawyer gave it to me. Pieter was very clear in his instructions. He said to give it to Wiliken when it was time to pass on the coin."

He stared up at them. "I have no idea where the Shrinking Coin is. Did Pieter ever say anything to you, Wiliken? Or the lawyers?"

Wiliken shook his head.

Uncle Hoogaboom sighed. "The Riebeecks have always kept it hidden for us. Now the magic will die with me. I'm so sorry, Hector." He buried his face in his hands.

"Oh, now, Uncle," Hector said as he walked over to his uncle and patted his back. "You're not to worry on my account."

Beezel could swear Hector was relieved and was trying hard to hide it.

"I'm sorry, Hoogaboom," Wiliken said. "I wish there was something I could do. After all these years . . ." He didn't finish.

Uncle Hoogaboom tried to smile. "We'll still find the treasure, Wiliken," he said. "But you have to understand, I will be remembered as the Hoogaboom who didn't pass on the Shrinking Coin."

After Wiliken had opened the box and seen that it was empty, he had set it on the coffee table. Mimi picked it up and inspected it.

"It's very pretty, isn't it, Beez?" she said as she turned it in her hands. "It reminds me of something." She thought for a minute. "Oh, I know! It looks like that puzzle box that Uncle Antonio brought Dad from Tajikistan, doesn't it? Remember? You were the one who figured out how to open it."

Beezel's heart skipped a beat. "Let me see that box, Mimi." Mimi handed it to her.

She examined the box. It was covered in a floral pattern. Each of the flowers had a tiny circular centre. If it was a puzzle box, almost anything could be a button or a lever. Beezel carefully inspected each flower on the four sides of the box. Suddenly, she smiled. "Uncle Hoogaboom," Beezel said, "do you have a straight pin?"

Uncle Hoogaboom stood up and rummaged through his pockets. "Here's a jeweller's probe," he said as he took off the top and handed it to her. "It has a sharp end—be careful."

Beezel took the metal probe, placed the tip in the centre of the flower on the front lower left corner and pressed.

A drawer, shaped exactly like one of the engraved flowers, popped out from the bottom of the box. Inside it were some small pieces of paper rolled into a scroll.

"Uncle Hoogaboom!" Mimi yelled. "Beezel's found something!"

"Take them out, Beezel," Wiliken said. "Let's see what they are."

Beezel removed the papers and unrolled them. The top paper was a handwritten note. Beezel handed it to Wiliken.

"It's to me," Wiliken said. "From my grandpa." He read the note out loud.

Dear Wiliken,

If you are reading this, then something has happened to me. It now falls on your shoulders to retrieve the Shrinking Coin from its hiding place. The two other papers will lead the way. You'll need Mathias to help you get the coin. Once you do, give the coin to my dear friend, and tell him to keep it for ever.

Uncle Hoogaboom smiled. "He offered to do that many times, Wiliken. But I always told him I wanted to find the treasure first."

Hector leaned over the twins. "What are the other papers?" he asked.

Beezel carefully peeled off the next paper from the roll. It was a tiny map of a section of Amsterdam, drawn in the same hand as the note written to Wiliken.

Uncle Hoogaboom examined the paper. "There's my street," he said.

"There's your house." Beezel pointed to a tiny square along the Prinsengracht. "And there's the Noordermarkt!"

"That's the walking tour you took us on!" Mimi said to Uncle Hoogaboom. "Do you suppose Wiliken's grandpa hid the coin in one of the buildings?"

Beezel studied the drawing. "But what's this?" She pointed to the edge of the drawing where a canal or a wide street had been drawn straight across the map. "There's no canal there, is there, Uncle Hoogaboom?"

"No, there certainly isn't." While Uncle Hoogaboom studied the little map, Mimi unrolled the last paper.

"It's some kind of list," she said to them. "It looks really old."

Uncle Hoogaboom took the paper from Mimi. "Left along the timber twenty paces, right at the first air duct, forty paces, right at the charred beam, down the rope ladder. Straight ahead. Behind the marked brick."

"No offence to your grandpa, Wiliken," Hector

said, "but these are pretty terrible clues. How are we supposed to find the Shrinking Coin with a map of Hoogaboom's neighbourhood and some weird hokey-cokey instructions?"

Wiliken shrugged. "Beats me."

Beezel stood next to Uncle Hoogaboom and looked at the map. On one side of the nonexistent canal, the side that butted up against the neighbourhood, Pieter had drawn a small arrow.

"You know," Beezel said, "that canal with the arrow reminds me of a fortress wall."

"A wall!" Uncle Hoogaboom said, slapping his forehead. "*Domkop!* How could I be so stupid! It *is* a wall. A big white wall, eight feet high. And I know just where it is." He turned and marched out of his apartment. "Do you remember I said I had a surprise for you?" he called over his shoulder. "Come see!"

"Uh," Wiliken said, "am I the only one who hasn't seen a big white wall at the end of the street?"

Beezel and Mimi eyed each other and shrugged. "We haven't seen one either," Mimi said. "And we hiked all around there yesterday."

"Well, we'd better follow him," Hector said. "If there's one thing I've learned on this trip, it's that when it concerns my uncle, you don't know what to expect."

"He's going up the stairs," Mimi whispered as she followed him.

"He's going to his studio!" Beezel said as they passed Wiliken's landing and kept going up.

Uncle Hoogaboom fished around in several of his pockets before bringing out the key that unlocked the studio door. He reached inside the door and flipped a switch. "This is what I wanted to show you."

Beezel couldn't believe her eyes.

Chapter Sixteen

It's something Pieter and I worked on for years. I've been trying to put on the finishing touches," Uncle Hoogaboom said proudly. "Welcome to my favourite part of Amsterdam."

Uncle Hoogaboom's large studio was filled from one end to the other, and from one side to the other, with models. Models that had been built directly on to the floor exactly as if they were on streets. A blue fibreglass canal ran along the side of one wall, all the way to the back.

"That's the Prinsengracht, isn't it?" Beezel asked him, and he nodded.

Beezel and Mimi gingerly stepped inside, over the canal and into the market square of the Noordermarkt.

"There's the church we went in!" Mimi said,

pointing to a large building in front of them. They were giants; giants who could walk across the tiny inlaid square and touch the top of the Noorderkerk.

"It's just the shell of the church," Uncle Hoogaboom said apologetically. "I was hoping to have it all finished before I showed it to anyone." He closed the studio door behind them. "I don't want to let my little cat inside right now. You'll see why in a minute."

"Oh, Uncle Hoogaboom," Mimi said. "It's really beautiful."

Beezel was speechless. It was everything Uncle Hoogaboom had shown them on their walking tour. She gazed over the rooftops and saw the row houses that lined the wide Westerstraat. "It's amazing," she managed to say.

"We positioned the canal to run along the long wall of the studio. Since we couldn't put real water in our canal, we thought we might as well use it as a footpath to get back and forth to the houses," Uncle Hoogaboom said, pointing to the far end of his studio. "Up there is the Westerstraat, then the Anjeliersstraat, and a tiny bit of the Tuinstraat."

He turned to the twins. "You girls remember all these streets, don't you? The little café down from my house that we had dinner in? It's all here." He patted Wiliken on the back. "And so is your grandfather's house . . . no, it's *your* house now, Wiliken."

"Honestly, Hoogaboom," Wiliken said to him, "you should go to work in Hollywood."

Uncle Hoogaboom laughed. "Your grandfather and I had many happy hours here, building and furnishing these models."

"But," Hector said, "what has this got to do with the Shrinking Coin and the papers that the girls found?"

"It's the same section of Amsterdam that's on the map, Hector," Beezel said.

"Pieter was sending us up here to get the coin," Uncle Hoogaboom said. "And I think if we go down the Prinsengracht until we get to the Anjeliersstraat, then turn right and go to the far corner of the studio, we'll find out what that arrow is." He looked at Beezel and Mimi. "Wouldn't you say?"

The twins nodded in agreement. They filed down the canal, turned right at the second street and stopped as they reached the back corner.

"Do you see anything?" Hector said from the rear of their single-file line.

Beezel and Mimi peered around Uncle

Hoogaboom. "There," Beezel said, pointing to a support beam that ran from the ceiling to the floor. Attached to the bottom of the wooden beam was a six-inch-round metal medallion. The design on the front matched the flower on Wiliken's puzzle box. "Push the centre of the flower, Uncle Hoogaboom," she said.

Uncle Hoogaboom bent down and pushed the flower's centre. There was a click and the medallion popped away from the beam on one side, like a small door, revealing a tunnel behind it.

"Let's see," Uncle Hoogaboom said as he wrestled with his pockets. "I usually keep a couple in here . . ." He held something up. "A flashlight." He shone it inside the tunnel.

"Can you see anything?" Mimi asked him.

Uncle Hoogaboom stood up and turned to face them. "No. I think it's time for the instructions you girls found." He unrolled the other small paper that had been in the box and handed it to Wiliken. "You'll have to go inside and get the Shrinking Coin, Wiliken." He smiled. "And *that* is why Fieffie can't be inside the studio right now."

"Seriously?" Wiliken broke into a grin. "You mean you're going to shrink me?" He put his fist in the air. "Yes! This is better than any vacation I've been on." He took the flashlight Uncle Hoogaboom handed him. "Shrink away!"

"Uncle," Hector said from behind Wiliken, "I think I should go, too." He leaned around Wiliken's tall frame. "He might need some help with those Dutch instructions."

"Well, then, take this," Uncle Hoogaboom rummaged inside another pocket and took out another flashlight.

"Oh, please, Hector," Mimi said, her hands clenched under her chin. "Can we go, too? *Please?*"

"We'd really like to," Beezel said. "And we won't get in the way . . ."

"And we'll mind you," Mimi added.

Hector turned to the girls. "Ah now, ducks, I don't know about this . . ."

"It *is* a once-in-a-lifetime opportunity, Hector," Uncle Hoogaboom said. "There won't be another chance for them to go inside this old house. And when you come back out, the girls can look around the models while we take care of transferring the Shrinking Coin."

"Yes!" Mimi squealed. "Please, please, please!"

Beezel crossed the fingers on both of her hands.

She had been ka-poofed hundreds of times, but this would be different. She would be herself, in her own body, just very little. She really did want to experience it.

Hector relented. "Only if you do *exactly* what I say."

"We promise!" the twins shouted together.

"I'll help look out for them," Wiliken said as he smiled at them. "Heck, these two are starting to feel like the little sisters I never had!"

Beezel looked at Mimi. Mimi looked at Beezel. The two girls sighed sadly in unison.

"Very good," said Uncle Hoogaboom. "Now stand still until you have all been zuufted. We don't want any accidents."

He pointed to Wiliken. Zuuft. He was about six inches tall.

He pointed to Beezel. Zuuft. Hector. Zuuft.

He was about to point to Mimi when she said. "Wait!"

Uncle Hoogaboom lowered his hand. "What's wrong?"

"I'm allergic to ka-poofing—it makes me itch like crazy," Mimi said. "So after you zuuft me, if I itch, will you un-zuuft me really fast?"

"I promise," Uncle Hoogaboom said. Zuuft. Mimi shrank down to the same size as Beezel—about the size of a hamster standing on its hind legs.

"Do you feel okay?" Uncle Hoogaboom asked her, his finger poised to unshrink her if needed.

Mimi waited a minute, then a big grin crossed her face. "Hey, I feel fine." She twirled. "*Finally* I get to experience the magic of a coin without itching!" Mimi hugged her sister. "Isn't this great, Beez? We're itsy-bitsy!"

They walked around Uncle Hoogaboom to the opened tunnel.

"Wait," Uncle Hoogaboom said as he took something out of his top left pocket. "Take this with you. I'll tie one end of it here to the medallion. Uncoil it as you go, so you won't get lost."

"Just like breadcrumbs," Beezel said as she took the ball of string Uncle Hoogaboom's giant hand set down on the floor in front of her.

"I'll wait for you in a chair by the studio door," Uncle Hoogaboom said. "All this excitement has worn me out, I must say. Be careful and come back soon. I'd hate to take the house apart to find you, but I will if I have to."

Wiliken turned on the flashlight and hurried

inside the tunnel. "Come on, you guys," he said. "Let's get that coin."

Beezel and Mimi unrolled the string behind them as Hector read the directions and Wiliken led the way. They went left along the timber for twenty paces and turned right at the first air duct. They walked forty paces and turned right at the charred beam. They came to a rope ladder that descended into a dark shaft in the wall.

Wiliken pushed up his sleeves and stuck the flashlight in his back pocket. "Let me do this," he said happily. "I live for this stuff." He climbed down the ladder. Hector shone his flashlight down the shaft to light his way. Beezel and Mimi leaned down and watched.

"Do you see it?" Mimi shouted after him.

"It's right here behind a brick," Wiliken said. "In some kind of canvas backpack. Man, this thing is really heavy. It will take me a minute to pull it out and put on the pack. Then I'll be right up."

Beezel breathed a sigh of relief as Wiliken's blond head appeared from the shaft. He climbed up on to the beam they were standing on and heaved the backpack on to the ground.

"Well," he said. "Let's take a look at it."

Wiliken pulled a bronze coin out of the bag and propped it up. The coin was about the size of an extra-large pizza to them. "It's solid," Wiliken said. "It feels like about eighty, maybe ninety pounds. That's a little more than I usually carry on my backpacking trips, but I can carry it out of here."

"Wow," Mimi said softly. "It's amazing."

"I wish Simon could be here," Beezel said as she ran her hand across its surface.

It was bronze, just like the Changing Coin. There were five words carved in a circle on one side. Wiliken turned the coin over. A design had been stamped into its surface. It was the image of two people standing side by side, one very small, the other larger. Around the outer edge of the coin were twelve tiny stars, each one with a ray that pointed to the image of the two people.

"The shrinking rule of twelve," Beezel said.

"I bet Hoogaboom is going to be happy to see this again," Wiliken said. "And think of it, Hector, the magic is going to be yours very soon now."

Hector made a kind of gulping sound. "Yes . . . I . . . I . . ." he stuttered. "I'm very . . . excited."

Beezel and Mimi looked at each other and grinned. Hector was nervous, but Beezel knew that after he had used the magic a few hundred times, it would feel as normal to him as combing his hair or brushing his teeth. He just had the jitters.

"Well, let's get going then." Wiliken wrestled the coin back into the canvas backpack and heaved it on to his back with Hector's help. "Okay, girls, let's follow that string!" He took the end from Mimi and began walking along its length.

The twins brought up the rear, wrapping the string into a ball as they walked. Beezel could see the light from Wiliken's flashlight dancing off the sides of the wall.

"Come on, you two!" Wiliken yelled. "Don't get too far behind us."

"Mimi, you're tangling up the string," Beezel said, stopping to make the coils neater.

"Why don't we just leave it here?" Mimi said. "It's just string. Uncle Hoogaboom can pull it out if he needs it."

"I suppose you're right . . ." Beezel stopped in midsentence.

Hector and Wiliken were yelling at something. The girls looked at each other, dropped the string and ran towards their voices.

"Beezel! Mimi! Quick!" Hector collided with the

twins as he came back to get them. "It's got Wiliken!"

The girls ran with Hector towards Wiliken's voice.

"Where is he, Hector?" Mimi asked frantically. The wooden beam was empty. The string lay slack on top of the timber. Next to it was the backpack with the Shrinking Coin, and Wiliken's flashlight.

"He's over there!" Hector turned his flashlight's beam down the passage. Beezel saw an enormous black rat. It had grabbed Wiliken by his pants leg and was dragging him deeper into the darkness. Wiliken slammed his fists against its side, but the rat seemed unaffected.

I hope ka-poofing works while I'm shrunk, Beezel thought as she raised her hand and pointed at the rat. "Keep your head down, Wiliken!" she shouted. Ka-poof. The rat was a beetle. It scuttled off as Hector and the twins rushed to Wiliken's side.

"Whew! Thanks," Wiliken said, his hand over his heart. "That was a close one. I dropped the pack when he came after me, thinking I could outrun him that way. But that rat had plans to make me his late-night snack."

"Did he bite you, Wiliken?" Beezel asked. "Check your leg and make sure the skin isn't broken."

Mimi held the light while they inspected Wiliken for teeth marks.

"It's just my pants," Wiliken said as he stood up. "No harm done."

"Oh, I'm so glad you're okay. Wil!" Mimi hugged him. Beezel felt that tiny pang again.

Wiliken ruffled Mimi's short hair. "Hey, I'm fine, kiddo."

"Let's get out of here," Hector said, nervously glancing around him. "That rat might have friends."

They helped Wiliken put on the heavy backpack, handed him his flashlight, and then followed Uncle Hoogaboom's string back to the opening in the studio wall.

Once inside the studio, Hector and Wiliken pushed the medallion closed, concealing the tunnel opening.

"That will keep any of his furry friends out of Hoogaboom's models," Wiliken said, brushing his hands together.

"Uncle Hoogaboom said he'd wait for us by the studio door," Hector said. "Let's go." He motioned to the girls. "Come along, ducks, don't dawdle."

"But you said we could look around a little," Mimi said. "We want to see the houses."

Hector studied the girls. "Oh, all right," he said. "You can go to the end of the studio. Stay on the Prinsengracht. Then turn right around and come back to the market square." He shook his finger at them. "But that's *it*. Don't you two go off exploring! I don't want to have to come looking for you."

"Thanks, Hector!" Beezel said. "We won't be long."

Their little band hurried down the Anjeliersstraat until they came to the Prinsengracht. Hector and Wiliken, carrying the Shrinking Coin, turned left towards the studio door where Uncle Hoogaboom was waiting for them. Beezel and Mimi turned right and lazily strolled down the street to where it butted up against the studio wall.

"Beezel," Mimi said, "I've been thinking about Wil."

"*Wiliken*," Beezel said as she felt the colour come back to her cheeks. If Mimi wanted to argue about him again, well, then, she would.

"You know . . ." Mimi twirled her hair as she walked. "Some day, Wil is going to be twenty-four and we'll be eighteen. That sounds a lot more reasonable, doesn't it?"

Beezel thought about it. "I guess it does, now that you mention it."

"So," Mimi said as she eyed Beezel carefully, "when we're eighteen, we could see who likes him more. And that way, we won't fight now."

Beezel stopped and grinned at Mimi. "Okay, we'll wait and see who likes him more in seven years. Whoever does, gets him."

Mimi put out her hand. "Deal." The twins shook hands. Beezel let out a deep sigh. At least she didn't have to worry about fighting over Wiliken again for seven years. That was a relief.

"I'd love to go inside this one," Mimi said as she ran up the steps of the last house and peeked in the window.

"Don't even think about it," Beezel said as she yanked her sister back down the stairs. "Remember what Hector said. We'd better go back."

They turned and headed back towards the Noordermarkt and Uncle Hoogaboom. While they walked, Beezel thought about the hidden treasure.

She wondered where Wiliken's grandpa had rehidden it. He had said that he put it in his den, but Wiliken had told them he and Uncle Hoogaboom had looked for weeks without finding anything. She sighed. And what did the old clue mean, anyway? Beezel ran over it in her mind.

> *Through walls like ice*
> *Past wood and metal*
> *Guarded by souls of sailors lost*
> *Lies the Spanish treasure*
> *Safe in Magda's capable hands*

They reached the part of the street where Uncle Hoogaboom lived. She saw the café on the corner where they had had dinner. She peeked inside the front window.

"Look, Mimi!" Uncle Hoogaboom had even placed the tables inside in the exact spots they were in the real café.

"You almost expect to see people eating inside," Mimi said.

They came to Pieter Riebeeck's house. Uncle Hoogaboom's red door with the sign on it that said HOOGABOOM'S ORIGINELE POPPENHUIZEN was there. The shop window on the ground floor that held his doll's furniture display was just the same as the real one.

Mimi whistled. "Uncle Hoogaboom even has

miniatures of his miniatures." She rubbed her forehead. "That kind of makes my head hurt."

Beezel stood in front of the house and thought about the two families. The Riebeecks and the Hoogabooms had gone through a lot together with the Shrinking Coin. And Uncle Hoogaboom and Pieter had tried so hard to find the treasure. If only it had been in the den like he said it would be. It would have made Wiliken and Uncle Hoogaboom so happy to find it. The only other thing that seemed to make Uncle Hoogaboom truly happy, besides treasure hunting, was model building.

Uncle Hoogaboom's models! Beezel grabbed Mimi's arm. "Mimi, I just thought of something!"

"What?"

"Remember what Pieter wrote to Wiliken in his letter?"

"He said the treasure was in his den . . . which it *wasn't*." Mimi sighed. "Oh well, maybe Fieffie ate it."

"And then he wrote that little thing." Beezel scrunched up her face. "What was it? 'The greatest treasures are in the smallest pleasures.'"

"Whatever." Mimi snorted. "A lot of help *that* was."

"Think about it, Mimi. Where did Uncle Hoogaboom and Pieter both love to spend time?"

Mimi thought for a minute. "You don't think?" She stared at Beezel and her eyes widened. "But he said it was in the den." Her eyes widened even more. "You think he hid the treasure in *there*?" She pointed to Uncle Hoogaboom's model house.

Beezel nodded. "It makes sense. He'd have a den in the model that was just like the one he had at home, wouldn't he?" She was getting excited now. "And the treasure would fit right in, wouldn't it? The greatest treasure would be hidden in their smallest pleasure!"

Mimi jumped up and down. "Let's go in! Come on!" She put her hand on the doorknob.

A loud crash and the sound of two men bellowing at each other caused Mimi to drop her hand and the two girls to turn towards the studio door.

"What on earth is *that*?" Mimi asked, looking down the Prinsengracht towards the source of the uproar.

"Let's go see!" Beezel grabbed Mimi's hand and the twins raced down the street.

When they reached the Westerstraat, Beezel

pulled Mimi behind a stoop. "Listen!" she told her twin.

"Make sure you tape his hands," a man's voice said. "And keep his fingers pointed down. Or you'll find yourself turned into a flea, or a rock."

"It was a *clam*," Mimi whispered. "That sleazeball has got to be Slear."

"I've completely taped his arms to the chair," another man said sarcastically. "I really don't think we have to worry."

"That's Edwin," Beezel said.

"Hector! Wiliken! Girls!" Uncle Hoogaboom shouted. "They've tied me up! Run!"

"For Pete's sake! Gag the old guy, Edwin," Slear said. "Although it's good to know those little girls are in here. We're going to have to be careful."

"Look!" Edwin shouted over the muffled cries of Uncle Hoogaboom. "It's Riebeeck!"

"He's been shrunk!" Slear yelled. "There he goes! Grab him! Blast it! He got away." He burst out laughing. "Did you see him? He's the size of a rat!"

"Slear, did Hoogaboom say those twins are inside here?" Edwin said.

"Keep your shorts on. Let me take a look." Slear sounded irritated.

The twins hid behind the stoop and listened as Slear made his way across the studio. "I don't see them," he said. "I'll bet they're shrunken, too."

There was silence, and then Edwin spoke. "Those twins are in here with us *and* they're *shrunken*?" He sounded afraid. "This is more than I signed up for. I won't be able to see them coming. Those girls could change me into a stray cat and leave me to wander the streets of Amsterdam."

"Good idea," whispered Mimi.

"Listen, pal, we're in this together," Slear said. "And if you don't help me, I don't care what your little piece of paper says, it's all gonna be m-i-n-e, mine."

The twins looked at each other. "We seriously have to ka-poof them," Mimi said.

Beezel nodded in agreement.

Another loud clatter caused both girls to flinch. "I got one of them!" Slear said. "He's under the bucket!"

A scuffling noise followed.

"Now, that's enough of that, you old geezer," an angry Slear said. "Edwin! Stop hiding like a coward and get over here! Tape his legs to the chair. He kicked over the bucket and let the little white-haired guy out."

"Hector!" Beezel's hand flew to her mouth.

"Don't worry, he got away from them, Beez." Mimi patted her shoulder.

They heard an ominous click as someone closed the studio door.

"Now they can't get out of this room," Slear said. "Come on, Edwin. We'll grab star boy and the other guy, and if we have to, we'll just leave those girls here with the old man." He laughed. "Can you imagine? We could bring the press gang back in here and let *them* find them. I'll film the whole thing. Oh, oh, and how's this? What if they hocus-pocus one of the guys on camera? Now, *that* would be news at eleven!"

Mimi turned to her sister. "Beez, that creep wants to *film* us ka-poofing some reporter!"

Beezel heard a rumbling sound, followed by a tremor. She peeked down the street and saw the front of a row house leaning back and forth in a dizzying way.

"You flush them out like this, see? And I'll bag 'em!" Slear shouted. "Hey, there goes one now! Grab him!"

The twins eyed each other and listened as Edwin and Slear moved down the Prinsengracht, shaking each of the row houses in turn.

They crept out from behind the stoop. "I can't see them, can you?" Mimi asked.

"I think Edwin is hiding behind the models," Beezel said as she looked up. "And I don't see Slear anywhere."

"*Now* what are we going to do?" Mimi asked her.

"I don't know," Beezel said as she saw a section of the roof from a model a few doors down crash into the street. "But we'd better get out of here."

The twins raced back to Uncle Hoogaboom's shop, opened the door, dashed inside and slammed the door behind them. It grew silent outside, and Beezel's heart sank. Maybe Edwin and Slear had caught Hector and Wiliken. What if they had? Would they just leave the twins here while they went to the press with their find? If so, it would just be a matter of time before reporters flooded Uncle Hoogaboom's studio and found two shrunken eleven-year-old magicians hiding in a model.

"Boy, are Mom and Dad going to be mad when they hear about this," Mimi said as she tried to catch her breath.

Beezel nodded in agreement.

"What should we do?" Mimi asked.

The crashing and bashing had started up again

down the street. Beezel sighed with relief. That could mean they *hadn't* caught Wiliken and Hector.

"Let's go upstairs," Beezel said. "Maybe we can find a spot with a good view and see what's going on."

"Good idea," Mimi said. The twins ran up the first flight. Beezel stopped on Wiliken's landing.

"Mimi," she said. The curiosity was killing her. Was she right about Pieter's clue? "Maybe we should just take a quick peek in the den."

"I was hoping you'd say that!" Mimi said as she opened the door. "We'll go fast!"

The twins raced down the hall to the den and opened the door. Everything was the same as it was in the real house. They quickly inspected the bookshelves for treasure chests. They checked the desk drawers and under the furniture. Nothing. Outside, they could hear Edwin and Slear's shaking edging closer.

"Let's go," Beezel said as she grabbed Mimi's hand.

But the twins froze when they heard a new sound: feet trudging up the stairs. The footsteps plodded down the hallway. The girls watched the den door.

"Hey! You're all right!" Wiliken said as he rushed over, dropped the pack that held the coin on to the floor with a thud and enveloped them in a big hug. "I thought you might come to Hoogaboom's shop. I was really worried about you two!"

"Where's Hector?" Beezel asked. "Is he okay?"

Wiliken ran his hands through his hair and leaned against the fireplace to catch his breath. "I'm sure he's fine. Hoogaboom got him out of the bucket, and he went running off into the models. Then they spotted me and I had to sneak through a few of the row houses. But I'm positive Hector got away from them."

"We were so worried," Mimi said.

The rumbling sound of the rocking models stopped again. In her mind, Beezel imagined that Edwin and Slear were moving down to the next building, just that much nearer to where they were.

She listened to Wiliken and Mimi as they quickly tried to come up with a plan of action. Her eye caught sight of something on the fireplace mantel directly behind Wiliken. There, in the centre of the shelf, was a glass case. Sitting inside it, on an ornately carved wooden stand, was what appeared to be a model of a ship.

There was something special about the model; it was so intricately made. Beezel tried to understand what it was about the ship that she found so fascinating. Then she knew. The reason she couldn't take her eyes off of it was because it was so . . . *realistic*.

For just a moment, Beezel couldn't talk. But her face must have shown her excitement, because Mimi immediately began to ask questions.

"What's wrong?" she said. "Are you okay?"

Beezel pointed to the fireplace. Was she right? It *did* fit the clue that Wiliken's father had left them. *Through walls like ice . . .* That could be the glass case. *Past wood and metal . . .* The ship itself. *Guarded by souls of sailors lost . . .* She supposed some sailors on both sides could have died when Koen Riebeeck's crew took over the Spanish ship.

"That's a happy look, right?" Mimi tried again.

Beezel managed to move her head up and down. Was it possible? Had Uncle Hoogaboom's relative shrunk the *entire* ship? Was *that* why it disappeared in the harbour all those years ago?

Maybe the treasure never left the very place the Spanish had put it!

She stared at the ship. It *looked* like a galleon. It

had the foremast at the front, and the mainmast behind it. A long raised deck went from the mainmast to the rear of the ship. At the stern of the ship, on top of this deck, was an even higher deck. Beezel knew from a report she had written in the fourth grade that it was called the poop deck.

But whether or not it was a Spanish galleon, and whether it was truly a shrunken treasure ship, she couldn't tell for sure.

Beezel moved around Wiliken and approached the glass box that held the ship. She gasped.

There, inscribed on a small silver plaque attached to the wooden stand that held the ship, was the word *Magdalena*.

It's safe in Magda's capable hands, Beezel thought to herself.

Wiliken touched Beezel's shoulder. "There's no time for admiring Hoogaboom's trinkets, kiddo," he said. "We've got to get out of here."

For the first time since she had met him, the words tumbled out of her mouth without the least bit of effort on her part.

"Wiliken, it's the treasure," she said as she pointed to the silver plaque. "There's *Magda*. It's the stand that's been holding the treasure ship. They didn't sink her, they *shrank* her. That's the Spanish galleon they brought into Amsterdam."

The rumbling of the models stopped and then started up again.

"Let's take a look," Wiliken said as he reached up and carefully took down the glass case.

"Hurry, Wil!" Mimi said. "It sounds like they're getting closer."

The box that held the ship was made from panels of glass that had been soldered together, just like a stained-glass window. Wiliken hurriedly made his way to a table on one side of the room and gently set the case down. Mimi and Beezel gathered around him.

"Here goes," he said. A small latch held the hinged top closed. Wiliken undid the latch and raised the lid. He gingerly removed the ship from its case.

In Wiliken's hands, the ship was the size of a large loaf of bread. If Wiliken had been his normal size when they had found it, Beezel guessed it would have looked more like a matchstick in the palm of his hand.

Wiliken placed the little ship on the table, holding it upright with his hands. "Let's see if I can spot anything inside the captain's cabin." He leaned down close to the small wooden ship and peered inside. "There's lots of stuff in there." He turned and stared at them in awe. "I think I see the captain's chest." Wiliken stood up. "It *is* our ship, I'm sure of it."

He positioned the ship back on the wooden stand inside the glass box. "She's a real beauty," Wiliken said. "You know, I'll have to talk to Hoogaboom about donating her to a museum." He closed and locked the glass case that held the little ship.

The loud boom of what sounded like a model being completely toppled startled the threesome. Beezel and Mimi clutched Wiliken's arms in fright.

"Okay, I don't know about you two," Wiliken said, "but I've had it with those guys. I say we ka-poof those two creeps before they rattle this model and damage our treasure ship *and* us. Then we'll find Hector." He looked at the bag on the floor. "I'll leave the coin here. That thing weighs a ton."

They ran down the stairs to Uncle Hoogaboom's front door. "Oh," Wiliken said, blocking the door. "Wait. I forgot to tell you something. Edwin has a trash can and Slear has a bucket. They want to catch us and start their very own miniature person zoo. So, you know . . ." He waved his hand in the air.

"Ka-poof first, ask questions later?" Mimi guessed.

"Exactly." Wiliken pointed at her.

As the twins followed Wiliken out of the shop, Beezel had only one thought in her head. She sure hoped both Slear and Edwin had bad aim.

Wiliken and the twins slinked along the edges of the models, towards the noise Edwin and Slear were making.

"Let's sneak back to the market square," Wiliken said. "You two can hide in one of the shops. Then I'll go out in the square and call Slear and Edwin. When they come to get me, you two can ka-poof them."

As they ran to the square, Beezel couldn't see Edwin or Slear anywhere, which made her very nervous indeed. She kept expecting to see a giant trash can or a bucket descend on her head at any moment. They dashed to the corner where the Westerstraat met the Prinsengracht.

They could see the market square, and the shell of the beautiful church Hoogaboom was building.

"In here," Wiliken said as he opened the door to the model of the small corner bookstore the girls had been to earlier with Hector. He hurried them inside. He pulled back the curtains and opened the front windows. "A perfect view! You two hide in here, and I'll get them to come out there." He pointed to the centre of the square. "That will give you a clean shot at them."

"Be careful," Beezel said. Her heart was beating hard.

Wiliken turned to them. "Listen, if they get me, you two stay put. I'm sure they'll want to go right out and announce their big scoop to the world. Then you two, quick as you can, find Hector and free Hoogaboom." He smiled and opened the door. "Okay, here goes nothing!"

The twins watched as Wiliken strolled out into the open.

"Slear!" Wiliken yelled at the top of his lungs. "Edwin!" Beezel and Mimi peeked up over the edge of the windowsill.

They could hear Slear yelling for Edwin to follow him as he trudged in their direction.

"He sounds like Godzilla," Mimi said. The twins watched Wiliken's face through the window. He was staring at the top of the building they were hiding in.

"Slear's getting closer," Beezel whispered. "I think he's in back of us."

Beezel and Mimi pointed out the window, ready to ka-poof the first person who set foot inside the square near Wiliken. But as they did, the walls and floor of the little bookstore began to shake violently. The front of the store lifted up.

"It's an earthquake!" Mimi shrieked as the shaking caused her to roll across the room and crash against the pine counter. The front door of the shop flew open and then slammed shut with a bang.

Beezel felt like she was in a storm at sea. The store tilted to the left and sent them tumbling. Then it tilted to the right, sending them sailing in the opposite direction. Beezel crawled to the window and peered out. They were off the ground! Beezel looked out into the square and saw that Slear had grabbed Wiliken. As she raised her hand to point at him, the store lurched to the right.

"Slear has Wiliken!" Beezel yelled as she tried to hold on to the windowsill. "And Edwin's picked up the bookstore! He's carrying us around!"

Books, magazines and the twins washed around inside the model as Edwin struggled to carry it.

"I've got the girls!" they heard Edwin yell at Slear. "I saw them! They're inside here. What should I do with them?"

Slear yelled back, "You'd better just lock the whole thing, kids and all, inside a closet! We'll figure out what to do with them later. And for Pete's sake, keep your hands away from the windows! You don't want those two pointing at you!"

The building settled into a rocking motion as Edwin edged his way across the studio, carrying the bookstore in his arms.

"Mimi!" Beezel called to her sister. "We'd better ka-poof Edwin soon, or we'll end up locked in Uncle Hoogaboom's closet!"

The girls grasped each other as they stumbled across the swaying room to the front window.

"Hold on to me!" Beezel said. Mimi grabbed Beezel around the waist and braced her feet against the wall under the window. Beezel leaned out on to a much higher panorama of Hoogaboom's models. It was as if they were in an Edwin-powered helicopter flying along at roof level.

"Oh, Beezel, I don't like this," Mimi whined.

"Listen," Beezel said. "Just hang on tight! I'm going to lean out a little farther and see if I can ka-poof him."

"Into what, Beez?" Mimi yelled at her. "If you change him into something little, the model might land on him and kill him *and* us! I know he's a bad guy and all, but that's pretty gross!"

"Great ogres and omelettes!" Beezel said. "You're right. And we'll need something that can hold the model." *Think . . . think . . . think*, she told herself. "Got it!" she said to her sister. "Here goes!"

Beezel leaned out the window as far as she could without falling out of the bookstore. She saw Edwin's knee and pointed. "Don't let go!" Ka-poof.

"Aaaah!" Beezel heard a terrified Slear scream. "Holy cow, Edwin! They've turned you into a gorilla!"

She could see Edwin's now hairy knee and one of his equally hairy feet. Beezel assumed he was still holding the model, since they hadn't crashed to the floor. That was a relief. And he was standing very still for the moment. But what would Edwin do next?

She turned to Mimi. "We'd better try to talk to him before he gets mad and smashes the bookstore, or gets scared and drops us."

181

The girls ran to the side of the bookstore, where they thought they might catch sight of Edwin the gorilla's arm or chest, and he would be better able to hear them.

A low grunting noise came from the top of the building. Beezel had a picture in her mind of Edwin's big gorilla head looming over the bookstore's rooftop.

She opened up a side window and yelled up, "Edwin! Set the bookstore down, right now! If you do, we promise we'll change you back! So set it down now, *gently*!"

Another series of deep grunts came from above them. Beezel thought he sounded like he was getting angrier. The bookstore suddenly tilted sharply to one side, sending the girls rolling across the floor, as Edwin began to walk.

"He's not listening, Beez," Mimi said as she helped Beezel up. The girls ran back to the window on the side of the building.

"Listen, Edwin!" Beezel yelled as loudly as she could. "If you don't put this bookstore down right now, we'll leave you like this *for ever*!"

"That's right!" Mimi shouted as she leaned out the window next to Beezel. "And if you do anything

182

to us, there won't be anyone left on the whole planet who can change you back into a person!"

Edwin stopped.

Beezel heard Slear yell, "Get out of my way, Edwin! I'm getting out of here!"

The twins ran back to the front of the store and looked out the window. Edwin was turning around. They could see the Noordermarkt square as it came into view. Then they saw Slear, almost at eye level, standing in front of them with Wiliken in his hand.

"Let's get him, Beezel," Mimi said quietly.

"Don't hurt me!" Slear spotted the twins glaring at him from the front window of the bookstore. "Listen, little girls . . ." His voice trembled as he held Wiliken out like some sort of talisman. "Just calm down now. Be good girls. Listen to reason. I've got your little friend here. We can work something out, right?" He laughed nervously and patted a kicking Wiliken on top of his head with a trembling hand. "After all, think of the headlines we could have with this one, right? We could all come out ahead with this story, am I right?"

Beezel cupped her hands around her mouth and yelled to Wiliken. "Wiliken! Hold on to Slear's hand! Hold on tight!"

Wiliken nodded.

"No!" screamed Slear. "Please, *please*, no more magic!"

Beezel pointed at Slear. Ka-poof. Slear was a Capuchin monkey.

Slear, now a twenty-inch-tall monkey, seemed genuinely surprised to see what appeared to him to be a much larger Wiliken in his hand. Wiliken prised the monkey's fingers off his waist and dropped to the floor. Then he took a few steps back, carefully watching Edwin the gorilla as he did so.

Noticing the fur covering his own hands and arms for the first time, Slear screeched in terror and headed for the shelter of the models.

Mimi tracked him with her finger as he ran. Ka-poof. Slear was a clam.

"Good one, Mimi," Beezel said. The sisters exchanged a high five. "And remember!" Mimi shouted down at Slear. "You're a *clam*, not a rock!"

"Are you guys okay?" Wiliken yelled up to them.

"We're fine!" Beezel shouted.

Edwin the gorilla began to slowly lower the bookstore to the floor. As soon as the model was deposited in the middle of the square, the girls darted out the front door. Beezel kept a wary eye on

Edwin as she followed her sister over to where Wiliken stood.

"I can't believe you're both okay!" Wiliken said as he gave them both a big hug.

"We're fine," Beezel told him. This was nice, getting hugged by Wiliken twice in one day. Beezel could smell his shampoo. It was a spicy smell, and very pleasant. But then she remembered Hector was missing. And poor Uncle Hoogaboom was taped to his chair with a gag in his mouth.

"Now what?" Wiliken motioned with his head towards Edwin the gorilla, who was standing very still behind the bookstore.

"He looks like King Kong," Mimi said.

Pulling back from their group hug, Beezel said, "I told Edwin we would change him back."

"Well . . ." Wiliken eyed the gorilla. "I think you might want to wait a little while. And I think you need to make him something a little bit smaller, just for our own safety."

"Make him a clam, too," Mimi suggested. "That way he won't wander off."

"I suppose you're right." Beezel pointed at the gorilla.

Edwin the gorilla covered his face with his hands.

Ka-poof. Edwin was a clam. In the girls' shrunken state, Edwin the clam appeared to be about the size of two large mixing bowls stuck together.

"Stay there!" Mimi commanded. "We'll be right back." She turned to Wiliken. "What should we do now?"

"Let's go help Hoogaboom first," Wiliken said. "And on the way we'll keep an eye out for Hector, okay?"

Beezel was beginning to worry. Where was Hector? She looked down the Prinsengracht. So many of Uncle Hoogaboom's models had been destroyed. And it was too quiet.

But then a small sound broke the silence. It was a little sound. A metallic tinkle, coming from the direction of the church.

"*Now* what?" Wiliken said.

Beezel's throat closed. She couldn't answer him. She knew exactly what that sound was. She had heard it the first time she had come to Uncle Hoogaboom's shop.

Mew.

Mimi looked at Beezel and her eyes widened in fear.

"Yep," Beezel said. "It's her." When Edwin and

Slear had come inside the studio, they had let Fieffie the cat in.

"Not Fieffie!" Wiliken pushed them inside the nearest house and closed the door, leaving just a crack to peek through. "Let's stay in here for a minute. I don't want her sneaking up on us—and I don't want to end up as cat chow."

"But what about Hector?" Beezel said.

"Shh, wait, listen," Wiliken interrupted. "Do you hear something?"

"I don't hear anything," Mimi said.

"Listen carefully," Wiliken said. "It's coming from the same direction as Fieffie's bell. It's a high-pitched sound . . . like . . . like . . ."

"Like someone is screaming!" Beezel opened the door and raced towards the sound of Fieffie's bell. As she ran, it occurred to her that the first time she had met the cat, it had been chasing her. Now she was chasing it.

She heard someone yelling. It was coming from the church! Beezel dashed across the market square to the unfinished model and through the opened front doors.

"Hector?" she yelled. "Are you in here?"

"I'm up here above the scaffolding!" Hector

answered. "This cat has me trapped in the choir loft!"

Wiliken and Mimi ran in after Beezel. "Where is he?" Mimi said.

They looked up. The inside of the building was under construction. It was an intricate framework consisting mainly of exposed wooden beams and columns. But there was one area of the choir loft that was semi-finished. A ladder led straight up to an opening in the platform. Every now and then, Beezel caught sight of a large cat's paw swiping across it.

"Hector!" Wiliken called up to him. "I'll climb up the scaffolding and draw her out!"

"Don't do it, Wiliken!" Hector said. "She's a fast one. She almost took my shirt off when she chased me up here!"

"We'll come up and ka-poof her!" Beezel yelled up.

"No!" Hector yelled. "She's waiting right by the entrance there. If you climb up, you're done for!"

"Where are you, Hector?" Mimi yelled. "Are you safe?"

"I crawled behind a stack of lumber," he shouted down. "She can't get her claws in here. I'll be fine.

188

Just leave me and go help my uncle. Then he can come get his blasted cat out of here!"

"I think he's right," Wiliken said to the twins. "It's the safest thing to do."

"Hurry, Beez!" Mimi said as she tugged Beezel's sleeve. "Let's go get Uncle Hoogaboom."

But Beezel knew exactly what it felt like to be trapped by Fieffie. She remembered the terror she had felt, and didn't want to leave Hector there a second longer. Besides, what if Fieffie found a way to get to him? She shuddered at the thought.

"No, Mimi," Beezel said. "I'm going to climb up and ka-poof that cat." She started towards the scaffolding.

Mimi grabbed Beezel's arm. "Hey, wait! I have a great idea!" She slipped off her backpack and took out the small plastic container. She opened it up and carefully spilled the ladybird into her hand.

"*Gumdrop*?" Beezel said. "But what if Gumdrop un-ka-poofs to the same scale as us? She would look like a little worm to Fieffie. That won't scare her."

"Don't be silly. Of course she won't look like a worm," Mimi said smugly. "She'll change back to her *original* form. That's how the magic works. She'll be five *feet* long when Fieffie sees her."

"You know what?" Beezel said slowly. "I think

189

you're right!" She looked at Mimi with admiration. "Good thinking."

"Uh, guys, what exactly *is* Gumdrop, originally?" Wiliken asked.

"A boa constrictor," Mimi said.

"*A boa constrictor?*" Wiliken ran his hands through his hair. "Well, I've got to give you girls credit, you aren't boring."

"I think we'd better find a hiding place," Beezel said. "Because if Mimi's right, Gumdrop is going to be one *big* boa constrictor."

"Gumdrop," Mimi told the bug, "you know how much you love to tease cats." She held her up. "There's one right up there, sweetie. See her? Go give her a good scare."

Mimi set the ladybird down on the floor and pointed at it. Ka-poof. The gigantic boa constrictor that writhed across the floor in front of them looked to Beezel like an undulating oil pipeline.

Wiliken, Mimi and Beezel quickly hid behind a half-built wall.

"Hector!" Mimi cried out. "Don't worry! Gumdrop is coming to save you!"

"GUMDROP?" Hector yelled back. "Oh, that's just fine! That's just *peachy*!"

The big snake spotted the motion at the top of the platform. She wound herself around the scaffolding and started her slow circular climb towards Hector and Fieffie.

Beezel winced as the big snake's head got near the opening. The end of Fieffie's tail flicked in and out, in and out.

"Oh dear," Mimi said. "Gumdrop really doesn't like anything waved in front of her face."

The snake nipped the cat's tail. The cat yowled and turned to face her attacker, teeth and claws bared. But at the sight of Gumdrop, it was as if a bolt of electricity shot through the cat's body. She leaped over the snake's head and flew all the way down to the floor. Fieffie was out of the church before Gumdrop could turn her head to watch her.

"Um, Mimi," Beezel said, pointing up, "Gumdrop is going into the opening where Hector is."

"I'd better ka-poof her," Mimi said nervously. "But I don't want her to fall, or fly away, or eat any of us . . ." She twirled her hair.

Beezel watched more and more of Gumdrop disappearing into the opening.

"What should she be . . .?" Mimi's voice drifted off.

"MIMI!" Hector yelled. "Get this snake out of here right now!"

"Hector! You know I can't *think* when you're yelling at me!" Mimi yelled back. She chewed on her lip.

Wiliken tried to help. "How about a camel?"

Mimi shook her head.

"A fox . . . a porcupine?"

Mimi shook her head and twirled her hair faster.

"A slug," Beezel said as she pointed to Gumdrop. Ka-poof. The snake changed into an enormous slug. To their shrunken group, Gumdrop seemed to be a two-foot-long tube of moving slime. The slug made its way slowly into the opening.

"Wow, that's one hefty slug," Wiliken said. "How come it's so big?"

"Well, I guess the ka-poofing magic can only change Gumdrop into an animal that is on the same scale that she is," Beezel explained. "Mimi ka-poofed Gumdrop back to her original size, which looks huge to us while we're shrunk. When I changed her into a slug, the slug is the size it would be in relation to Gumdrop, not us."

"Wow," Wiliken said. "You're pretty smart,

aren't you, Miss Beezel?" He playfully punched her in the arm.

Beezel blushed and stammered, "S-s-sometimes."

"I'll be right there, sweetie!" Mimi called as she started to climb up the scaffolding. She stopped, glanced down over her shoulder to Beezel and smiled triumphantly at her. "See? I *knew* I should bring Gumdrop along. If it weren't for Gumdrop, Fieffie would have *eaten* Hector."

Beezel shook her head and marvelled once again at her sister's logic concerning her pet boa.

"Hey," Wiliken said as he watched Mimi climb the scaffolding. "Is it always like this with you guys?"

Beezel nodded and giggled. "Pretty much, yeah."

Mimi ka-poofed the two-foot-long slug into a ladybird the size of a small turtle. Wiliken climbed the scaffolding and helped Mimi carry Gumdrop safely to the ground. A shaken and relieved Hector appeared in the opening and began to make his way down as well.

While Beezel waited, she studied the interior of the church. She had never really thought about how Uncle Hoogaboom had made the models. She guessed there was a lot of cutting and gluing involved. But what she saw inside the church told her a different story.

It looks as if real people are helping to build this, she thought to herself. *Why would Uncle Hoogaboom need scaffolding at all? It just doesn't make any sense.*

Her eye caught sight of a bit of bright colour on the floor against one wall. She picked it up. It was a crumpled red hat, well worn and covered in sawdust. Inside the hat Beezel found a wadded-up sandwich wrapper.

Sawdust and sandwiches, Beezel thought. *Now, that's interesting.*

While they spent what felt like an hour untaping Uncle Hoogaboom from his chair, Beezel and Mimi took turns sitting on his shoulder and telling him about the treasure ship they had found inside the model of Pieter Riebeeck's house.

"Well, of course, that's what Pieter meant," Uncle Hoogaboom said. "He couldn't have been plainer. He said it was in his den, didn't he, Wiliken?"

"He just didn't say which one," Wiliken shouted up to Uncle Hoogaboom as he wrestled with the sticky tape Edwin had used to bind his arms to the chair.

After they untaped his legs, Uncle Hoogaboom gratefully stood up and stretched. "Well, that was a close call all around, wasn't it?" he said as he peered down at the diminutive group at his feet. "Would you like me to unshrink you now?"

Beezel remembered something. "We left the treasure ship and the Shrinking Coin inside your house," she shouted up at him. "Your *little* house," she corrected herself.

"Don't forget the clams," Mimi reminded her.

"Oh, that's right." Beezel pointed behind her towards the corner of the Westerstraat. "They're over there."

"Why don't you unshrink the girls first, Hooga-boom?" Wiliken yelled. "Hector and I will go get the treasure ship and the Shrinking Coin." Hector and Wiliken headed down the Prinsengracht together.

"Ready?" Uncle Hoogaboom asked the girls. "Stand well away from each other. Farther." He waved the twins apart.

"Wait!" Mimi yelled. She gathered up Gumdrop the ladybird and carried her to the far edge of the market square. "I don't want to squish her when you un-zuuft me."

Uncle Hoogaboom pointed to Beezel. Zuuft. Beezel was herself again. He pointed to Mimi. Zuuft. Mimi was her normal size again, too.

Mimi pointed to Gumdrop on the floor. Ka-poof. Gumdrop was a five-foot-long boa constrictor again. Mimi picked her up and draped her around her shoulders. "You did a great job today, Gumdrop."

Wiliken, carrying the coin in the backpack, and Hector, holding the glass case that contained the Spanish galleon, approached Uncle Hoogaboom and the twins.

"Your turn now?" Uncle Hoogaboom asked them.

"You'd better take this first, Uncle!" Hector yelled as he held out the shrunken treasure ship.

Uncle Hoogaboom lowered his hand to the ground, and Hector set the glass case on his palm. "You know, Hector, I think I'm going to call the ship *Magdalena*," Uncle Hoogaboom said as he stared at the tiny galleon in his hand, "since that's what it said on her stand."

Hector helped Wiliken hold up the Shrinking Coin. "Take this, too, Hoogaboom!" Wiliken called.

Uncle Hoogaboom reached down, plucked the coin from Wiliken and Hector's hands and put it in his pocket.

"There now," Uncle Hoogaboom said. "Are you two ready?"

Hector and Wiliken nodded.

"Move apart," Uncle Hoogaboom said. "Leave some room between you for unshrinking." He nodded. "There, that's enough."

Zuuft. Zuuft. Hector and Wiliken were full size again.

"That was an amazing journey, Hoogaboom," Wiliken said as he hugged the old man. "Thank you for that."

"Yes," Hector said. "I can truthfully say I've never been through anything like it."

Mimi walked over to the two clams and picked them up. "I've got the bad guys," she said. "What are we going to do with them?"

"Clam chowder comes to mind," Hector muttered. The twins giggled.

"Hmm," Uncle Hoogaboom said. "I have a storage closet we can lock them in. It will keep them out of harm's way, just until we get a chance to call the authorities."

"Uncle," Hector said. "About the Shrinking Coin . . ."

"Oh yes, yes," he said, fishing in his pocket and bringing it out. "Let's take care of that right now!"

Hector put his hand on his uncle's arm. "Let's wait."

"Wait?" Uncle Hoogaboom gave him a puzzled look. "But nephew, it's time for me to pass this on. I thought I'd explained, I'm getting old . . . and . . ."

"No, let's just wait"—Hector interrupted him, and smiled—"until after *you* unshrink the treasure ship."

Uncle Hoogaboom grinned. "Thank you, Hector." He turned to them. "So, should we see her full size now?"

"Yes, I can't wait to see it!" Mimi said, bouncing on her feet.

"We'd better go outside first," Wiliken said. "That ship is going to be pretty big when you make it full size again. Where can we do it?"

"Maybe we can unshrink her in the canal," suggested Beezel.

"That's a good idea," Uncle Hoogaboom said, carefully holding the ship in his hand. "But first," he said as he opened the door to his studio and

198

stepped out on the landing, "let's lock those clams in a closet."

Uncle Hoogaboom searched in his pockets with his free hand and pulled out a key. Across the landing was a door. He unlocked it and flipped on a light. Inside the rather chilly closet were a bucket, a mop and a broom. "It's nice and cool in here," Uncle Hoogaboom said. "This should do fine."

Mimi took the two clams and placed them in the bucket.

"Behave yourselves," Uncle Hoogaboom said as he closed the door and locked it. "We'll be back to get you later."

They hurried down the stairs and into Uncle Hoogaboom's shop.

"Uncle Hoogaboom," Beezel said, "I've been thinking. How are we going to get a one-inch-long galleon out into the centre of the canal? The tiniest wave will capsize it."

"I hadn't thought of that." He stroked his beard in thought.

Hector scratched his head. Wiliken stared off into space with a puzzled expression on his face. And Mimi stared at Beezel while she twirled her hair.

Beezel stood with her hands on her hips and

tapped one foot. After a few minutes, she had it. "Hey, I've got an idea. What if we built a raft? We could float the *Magdalena* into the centre of the canal, and then you could un-zuuft her."

"That's a good idea, Beez," Mimi said. "But where are we going to get the wood for a raft?"

"Right here in Uncle Hoogaboom's detail room," Beezel said. "I'll bet you have shrunken planks, don't you, Uncle Hoogaboom?"

"A raft!" Uncle Hoogaboom smiled. "Of course I have lumber. All sizes!" He snapped to attention. "Wiliken, hold the *Magdalena* for me." Uncle Hoogaboom reached in his pocket and took out a pair of tweezers. While Wiliken held the case, Uncle Hoogaboom opened it and extracted the ship and its stand and placed them in the palm of his hand. He set the empty glass case on a shelf. "Hector, do you still have the flashlights I gave you to use inside the wall?"

"Yes," Hector said.

"Good. Here, Wiliken, you hold the *Magdalena*. And Hector, you hold the stand. I need to get a few other things." Uncle Hoogaboom rummaged around on a top shelf and popped several small wooden planks, no bigger than a ruler, into his pocket. "These will be good for a gangplank. We'll take this smaller piece for a raft, I think." He plucked a shorter piece of wood from the shelf and put it in his pocket as well.

"Hmm." Uncle Hoogaboom scurried over to a different shelf. "I must have one here somewhere," he muttered. Beezel saw tiny lanterns, ceiling fans and stained-glass windows. "Ah, here it is!"

He selected a rolled-up rope ladder and slipped it inside his pocket. "We should be able to hang it over the side of the ship. And we'll need some rope." He stuffed some threadlike bundles into his pocket with the lumber and ladder. "And I think . . . one rowboat."

Hoogaboom handed a rowboat, the size of a bath toy, to Beezel for her to hold.

"And something to break any locks we run across." Uncle Hoogaboom plucked what looked to Beezel like a paper clip-sized crowbar off a different shelf and stuffed it in another of his bulging pockets.

"And I think, to be safe, we should secure the galleon to the raft," Uncle Hoogaboom said. He stopped at Gaidic's desk and grabbed a handful of drawing pins from inside her desk drawer. "That should do it. I'll unshrink everything outside." With that, he turned, opened his red front door and stepped outside into the crisp night air.

"Uncle Hoogaboom, don't unshrink anything without me!" Mimi called after him. "I'm going to put Gumdrop in your bathroom! It's too cold for her outside!" Mimi turned to Beezel. "Wait for me."

"All right, but hurry up!" Beezel said. Mimi ran down the hall with the big snake.

As Beezel waited, she glanced at her watch. It was almost midnight, which was good. She hoped there would be fewer people out and about.

After Mimi had safely secured Gumdrop in the bathroom, the twins rushed to join Hector, Wiliken and Uncle Hoogaboom at the edge of the canal.

Uncle Hoogaboom was scrutinising the areas to the left and right of the canal. "She should be about a hundred and forty feet long when I bring her back to her normal size," he said. "Wouldn't you say, Wiliken?"

"Yes," Wiliken said as he inspected the canal in front of them. "You've got plenty of room. There aren't any canal boats near us on this side."

"It's pretty quiet all around," Hector said, checking the street for pedestrians. "There are a few people down the street a ways, but I think if you're quick, they'll hardly notice in the dark."

"Then it's time," Hoogaboom said as he emptied his pockets. "Stand back." He lined up the ladder and planks on the ground in front of him and pointed. Zuuft. The ladder was full size. Zuuft. Zuuft. Zuuft. Zuuft. Three large wooden planks, and one shorter one lay next to it.

Next Hoogaboom took three bundles of rope from his pocket. Zuuft. Zuuft. Zuuft. "Very good," he said.

Uncle Hoogaboom grabbed the shorter plank of wood and walked over to Hector. "Put *Magdalena's* wooden stand in the centre of the plank," he instructed Hector as he set it on the ground. "Parallel to the length, and hold her steady."

Hector held the tiny stand while Uncle Hoogaboom secured it upright by placing a ring of drawing pins all around it. To Beezel, the drawing pins that held the ship's wooden stand in place looked like a colourful plastic fence.

"Wiliken," Uncle Hoogaboom said, "bring the ship here. Let's see if this holds her." Wiliken leaned down and carefully placed the *Magdalena* in her pinned wooden stand.

"Hector, hand Mimi one of the flashlights."

Next Hoogaboom grabbed a bundle of rope. Then he took the miniature rowboat from Beezel and, leaning over the side of the canal, placed it in the water. Zuuft. A full-size rowboat bobbed gently against the side of the canal. He secured one end of the rope to the front of the rowboat and handed the other end to Hector. Wiliken and Beezel reached down and held the boat against the canal's side.

"Now we'll put our little galleon out in the middle of the canal." Uncle Hoogaboom picked up the plank that held the treasure ship and carefully placed it on the bench of the rowboat. He climbed in the boat and sat beside it. "Give her a push out, Wiliken," he said. "Nice and gentle. We don't want any waves."

Wiliken told Beezel to push the rear of the boat into the canal. Then he gave the front of the boat a gentle push, sending it out into the still water.

When the rowboat reached the middle of the canal, Uncle Hoogaboom carefully placed the plank down into the water.

"Mimi!" Uncle Hoogaboom called. "Put the flashlight beam on her!" Mimi switched on the flashlight and pointed it at the floating platform that held the *Magdalena*. Now that it was illuminated, Beezel could just make out the tiny ship sitting safely inside its drawing pin fence.

"Now reel me in nice and slow, Hector," Uncle Hoogaboom said as he looked back at the treasure ship on its raft. Hector pulled on the rope that was attached to the rowboat, slowly drawing it closer. When the rowboat reached the canal's side, Uncle Hoogaboom climbed back up and stood next to them. He raised his hand and pointed at the ship, waiting for just the right moment.

"Now, Hoogaboom!" Wiliken said as the plank holding the tiny treasure ship turned in perfect parallel to the canal's banks.

Zuuft!

CHAPTER SEVENTEEN

It was the most splendid thing Beezel had ever seen. Waves lapped against the side of the canal as the ship settled into the waterway. She gazed up at its rigging, shimmering in the bright moonlight, and was speechless.

But Mimi wasn't.

"Can we go on board? Can we, Wil?" She tugged on his sleeve. "It's floating, so it's safe, right? Come on, let's go see the treasure!"

The treasure ship was still several feet away from where they stood on the side of the canal.

Uncle Hoogaboom pointed to the galleon. "Wiliken, I think you'll have to climb up the anchor cable."

Wiliken grinned. "That's just the kind of thing I like to do, Hoogaboom." He jumped down into the rowboat.

"Take these." Hoogaboom handed him two bundles of rope. "And this." He placed the rolled rope ladder in the bottom of the boat. "See if you can hang the ladder over the side. We can use it to get on to the ship."

Wiliken began to row the short distance to the side of the galleon.

"Be careful!" Beezel and Mimi cried in unison.

Beezel felt like she held her breath the whole time Wiliken was climbing the cable. When he reached the railing and pulled himself over on to the deck, she let her breath out and sighed in relief.

"This is incredible!" Wiliken called over to them. "I'll secure the ladder and come back to get you!"

Hoogaboom and Hector were the first two Wiliken rowed to the galleon's side. Hector yanked hard on the ladder. "Seems sturdy enough," he yelled at the twins, and then he began his climb up the ladder to the deck, followed closely by Hoogaboom.

Wiliken rowed back and got the twins. Mimi and Beezel, being used to ladders of all sorts back home in the circus, made fast work of getting on board the ship.

As they stood quietly together on the deck, Beezel

couldn't believe her eyes. She was standing on a ship that had once sailed to the Caribbean in the 1600s. Looking out at the historic row houses of Amsterdam, she could imagine what it must have felt like to sail into its harbour hundreds of years ago.

Mimi broke their silence. "Okay, now let's go find that treasure!"

Hoogaboom led them to the captain's cabin. With help from Wiliken and Hector, the three men pushed open the door. The air that greeted Beezel's nose smelled like time itself: a stale, worn-out smell.

They entered a small room. Uncle Hoogaboom turned on his flashlight and ran its beam around the cabin. To the left of the door on a wooden platform was the captain's bed. Against the far wall, beneath a window with a view out the stern of the ship, was a chest.

Beezel ran to it and inspected the lock.

"You'll need that crowbar," she said to Uncle Hoogaboom.

He nodded and rummaged inside his pocket with one hand while handing the flashlight to Wiliken to hold with the other. Placing the tiny metal piece on the floor of the cabin, he pointed. Zuuft. Uncle Hoogaboom grasped the full-size crowbar and handed it to Hector. "I'm afraid this is a younger man's job," he said.

Hector wedged the crowbar into the lock. Taking a deep breath, he pushed down, putting his full weight on to the bar. The lock popped open.

"Well," Uncle Hoogaboom tugged at his beard excitedly, "here goes, eh, Wiliken?"

Uncle Hoogaboom quickly removed the broken lock, and together, he and Wiliken opened the lid.

"Alakazam and alfalfa," Beezel said softly. "Would you look at that!"

Mimi reached down into the chest. She scooped up a handful of silver coins and let them fall through her fingers. "Wil, you and Uncle Hooga-boom are *rich*!"

Wiliken and Uncle Hoogaboom stood side by side and stared down at treasure.

"We did it, Hoogaboom," Wiliken said.

"Yes we did, son." Hoogaboom slapped him on the back. "The Hoogabooms and Riebeecks are always stronger when they work together."

CHAPTER EIGHTEEN

That morning, when the sun came up, and Uncle Hoogaboom's neighbours got dressed and ate their breakfast, they were greeted by the sight of a Spanish galleon in the canal outside their homes, where none had been the night before. A particularly concerned citizen, wondering if the ship had the proper permit to dock in the canal, had even called the police.

Wiliken and Uncle Hoogaboom were alarmed when they saw the crowd gathering by the canal next to the ship, but Hector, practised with years of being in the Trimoni Circus, didn't miss a beat.

"Did you two decide to donate the ship?" he asked Uncle Hoogaboom and Wiliken. They nodded. "In that case . . ." Hector took a deep breath. "In appreciation for all that the city of

Amsterdam has done for their families," Hector pontificated from the bow of the ship, his white hair waving in the gentle morning breeze, "Wiliken Riebeeck and Mathias Hoogaboom would like to donate this ship to the Scheepvaartmuseum!"

Beezel had read about that particular museum in the guidebook. It was Amsterdam's maritime museum. The *Magdalena* would find a good home there.

Uncle Hoogaboom provided a spirited translation and the crowd burst into applause. Hector even got them to pull the ship closer to the canal's side by tossing them ropes that he had lashed to the ship and instructing them, with Uncle Hoogaboom's help, to pull in unison.

When the enthusiastic crowd had towed the treasure ship close enough to the canal's edge and tethered it, the twins helped Hector and Wiliken use Uncle Hoogaboom's lumber to create a gangplank.

That's when several of the younger people who had gathered recognised Wiliken. He graciously signed autographs at the bottom of the gangplank while Hector acted like a guard at the top, refusing admittance to one and all.

"Sorry, folks, but until a few private effects have been removed, we can't allow any visitors on board," Hector said to the crowd, first in English, then more slowly in Dutch. "I'm sure you understand."

At the first opportunity, Uncle Hoogaboom ran across the street to his shop and called the Nederlandsche Bank. Then Wiliken, Hector, Mimi, Beezel and Uncle Hoogaboom leaned on the ship's railing and waited for the armoured truck Uncle Hoogaboom had requested to transport the millions of dollars' worth of gold, silver and jewels to the bank.

Beezel and Mimi got hungry while waiting for the bank truck and volunteered to make sandwiches for everyone.

"Besides, I need to check on Gumdrop," Mimi said.

When they entered the shop, they saw Gaidic, standing at the window with her hand to her mouth, staring at the ship.

"Morning, Gaidic!" Mimi sang as she headed back to Uncle Hoogaboom's apartment.

"Um, Hector's over there." Beezel pointed to the treasure ship sitting in the middle of the canal.

"It really *is* a Spanish galleon, isn't it?" Gaidic said.

"It is," Beezel said. "Don't worry, I'm sure Hector will explain everything." She ran after Mimi. "We'll be right there. We're bringing over some food to eat!"

When the twins brought the food back to the galleon, Gaidic was already on the deck of the ship, and she was asking questions.

"This has something to do with the treasure you've been talking about, doesn't it, Mathias?"

"Well, er, you could say that, yes." Uncle Hoogaboom fidgeted under her gaze.

"And you," she turned to Hector. "You knew something the other night, when those two"—she pointed to a sheepish Wiliken and Uncle Hoogaboom—"made me leave early."

"I did, and I'm sorry," Hector said. "Gaidic, could you wait right there just a minute?" He pulled Wiliken, Uncle Hoogaboom and the twins aside. "I want to tell her about the Shrinking Coin," he said.

"She must mean a lot to you, nephew," Uncle Hoogaboom said. "Maybe you should just *show* her how it works." He took the Shrinking Coin from his pocket and placed it in the palm of his hand. As Wiliken and the twins watched, Uncle Hoogaboom put Hector's hand over his, covering the coin. He leaned down close to Hector's face and whispered the five magic words in his ear.

"The magic and the coin are yours now," Uncle Hoogaboom said as he pressed the coin into Hector's hand.

Hector was too overcome with emotion to speak at first. After he cleared his throat several times, he said, "I expect you'll be helping me practise, Uncle, before I leave?"

Uncle Hoogaboom smiled and patted his back. "It would be my pleasure."

Once they were back inside Uncle Hoogaboom's shop, Beezel thought Gaidic adjusted fairly well to the realisation that there was such a thing as zuufting in the world. Having a private demonstration of Hector's new ability certainly helped.

"I'm just glad you are all okay," Gaidic said to them after she recovered from watching Hector zuuft and un-zuuft her desk several times. "To think I let them in the house, those bad men." She looked at the twins. "Pieter's cousin, that Edwin, told me he accidentally locked himself out of the building. He showed up on my doorstep with that other man, Slear. Edwin told me he had to get his luggage out very soon or he would miss his plane. He said no one was answering the door or the phone. I went back to the shop and let him in with my key. How was I to know he was a madman?"

After the bank personnel removed the treasure from the galleon, Uncle Hoogaboom hired a security company to guard the ship until the Scheepvaartmuseum was ready to receive it.

Uncle Hoogaboom and Wiliken had assured the curator that the entire ship could be moved overnight as long as they did it before Hector had to leave for home.

"Oh, does he fly a helicopter?" the curator had asked the twins.

"Something like that," Beezel said.

Later that afternoon, Uncle Hoogaboom called the police and asked them to pick up Edwin and Slear from his home. Leaving Gaidic downstairs to direct the police, the rest of them trooped up the stairs to the studio landing. On the way up, Uncle Hoogaboom reminded Hector not to say anything about the transfer of the Shrinking Coin magic.

"Let's keep those two as confused as possible," Uncle Hoogaboom whispered as he came to the landing, "for as long as possible." He unlocked the door to the closet.

Mimi pointed to one clam. Ka-poof. Beezel pointed to the other. Ka-poof. Slear and Edwin stood staring at them.

Uncle Hoogaboom wagged his finger at them and said, "You two are going to go to jail. The police are on their way over here, now."

"Oh, I don't think so, old man," Slear said as he pushed Uncle Hoogaboom aside and started to run down the stairs.

Mimi pointed at his back. Ka-poof. Slear was a clam again. He bounced down three steps and sat spinning on the fourth.

"Some people never learn," Mimi said as she retrieved him. She brought Slear back up the stairs and set him down in front of Uncle Hoogaboom. Ka-poof. Slear was himself. He staggered a little, as if he were still dizzy from spinning.

"Mimi, Beezel," Uncle Hoogaboom said as he scratched his beard, "I've been thinking. Maybe they both need another change or two. We don't want any more trouble from them."

"Sure." Mimi pointed at Edwin. Ka-poof. Edwin was a clam. Ka-poof. Edwin was Edwin.

216

"Stop! I get it!" Edwin pleaded. "No more, please!"

"Your turn." Beezel pointed to Slear. Ka-poof. Slear was a clam. Ka-poof. Slear was Slear. "Want to try running away again?" she said as she pointed at him. He shook his head.

"Listen, girls," Hector said thoughtfully. "Why take any chances with these two? What if they run off to the press with their little stories?" He waved a hand at them. "Just change them back into clams, and we'll tell the police they got away."

"NO! No . . . more . . . clams," Slear blubbered. He turned to Uncle Hoogaboom. "I'll be good this time, I swear. I won't say a word to anyone about anything." He pointed at Mimi and Beezel. "They didn't turn me into anything." He pointed at Uncle Hoogaboom. "You never shrank me." He waved his hand at Hector and Wiliken. "You didn't do anything either."

As long as Slear was making promises, Beezel had one she wanted him to make. "What about Wiliken?" she asked. "Are you going to stop hounding him? Huh?" She pointed at him.

"And calling me star boy?" Wiliken added.

"Sure, sure," Slear said, sobbing as he put up his hands. "No more. I swear it."

Beezel lowered her arm. "I hope you keep your promises, Mr Slear. Because if you don't, Mimi and I will come visit you."

Edwin stood very still, as if any movement on his part might cause someone to point at him with dire consequences.

"Well, Edwin," Wiliken said, "you've certainly clammed up." He elbowed the twins.

The twins laughed. "Good one, Wil," Mimi said.

Edwin cleared his throat. "I'll behave. I swear it," he whispered. "I just want *out* of this house. I won't do or say a thing to *anybody* ever again."

Hector winked at the twins and nodded with satisfaction.

Gaidic called up the stairwell, "*De politie is er, Mathias! Ze komen naar boven!*"

Uncle Hoogaboom told Wiliken and the girls, "She said the police are here, and they're coming up."

Two policemen came up to the landing and spoke to Uncle Hoogaboom in Dutch. He pointed to Edwin and Slear.

"What's he saying?" Beezel whispered to Hector.

"I think he said that they broke into his studio and damaged his models," Hector said.

218

Slear, overhearing Hector's translation, grabbed one of the officer's arms and said, "Yes, that's right, I broke in! I smashed everything! Now please, arrest me! Lock me up! Just get me out of here!"

After the police left with Edwin and Slear, Uncle Hoogaboom and Wiliken drove Hector, the girls and Gumdrop back to the Merlin Hotel. Mimi had changed Gumdrop back into a ladybird and put her in her plastic container for the ride over.

As Beezel gazed out the car window, she pondered a theory she had come up with. She had given a lot of thought to the Dutch gnomes called *kabouters*, the scaffolding in Uncle Hoogaboom's model and the tiny hat and sandwich wrapper she had found. She thought she knew what they all meant. It was time to see if she was right.

"Uncle Hoogaboom," Beezel said, "I know I saw a tiny man inside the doll's house room, and I was wondering . . . have you been shrinking people to help build the models? Is that who I saw? Someone like a construction worker?"

Hoogaboom smiled sheepishly at her in the rearview mirror. "Well, I can't be sure *exactly* who it was you saw. But it was one of my night crew."

"Your *night crew*?" Hector said.

"Yes, they are some friends who work for me." Uncle Hoogaboom held up one hand and wiggled his fingers. "My arthritis keeps me from doing as much of the finer work in the models as I used to. Pieter and I could do all the major building ourselves, but there were so many little things that were becoming more difficult with age. Things like installing banisters, or in the case of the church, finishing the choir loft. So, we hired some good friends to work on our models at night. I zuufted them at nine each night and un-zuufted them in the morning before Gaidic came to work. Sometimes a member of the crew would forget to turn up for the un-zuufting. They'd spend the day shrunk as well."

"Well, that sure explains the *kabouters*," Mimi said. "Doesn't it, Beez?" Beezel nodded.

"It wouldn't surprise me to find out that the Hoogabooms are responsible for all the *kabouters* in Holland," Hector said.

"Not *all*." Uncle Hoogaboom chuckled. "But it is a good thing I gave the crew the day off on Monday. I knew I would be having company that evening. I just didn't know it would include Edwin and Mr Slear. Happily, my good friends will never have to

220

work another day in their lives. There's plenty of money for all of them."

The rest of the week went quickly for the girls. Hector and Gaidic took them to the Rijksmuseum. Wiliken and Uncle Hoogaboom took them to the Rembrandthuis and the Van Gogh Museum again, as a special treat for Mimi. Then they drove them all out to the Keukenhof Flower Gardens to see the tulips, as a surprise for Beezel.

Uncle Hoogaboom and Wiliken came to each of the girls' magic shows their last weekend in Amsterdam. Before they knew it, Sunday had arrived and they would be leaving in the morning. It was just as Beezel had thought; the time had flown by.

Beezel and Mimi decided that they wanted to do a private magic show on the *Magdalena* Sunday night just for Uncle Hoogaboom, Wiliken, Gaidic and Hector. Uncle Hoogaboom managed to run an electrical cord from a neighbouring canal boat, and Gaidic found the girls some fairy lights to hang across the deck.

The girls took magic requests from Wiliken, Gaidic and Uncle Hoogaboom. Even Hector got into the act and shrank Uncle Hoogaboom, so he could experience the magic of the Shrinking Coin once before they left.

"I wish I had been on the night crew all these years myself," Uncle Hoogaboom said when Hector un-zuufted him after he had explored the ship's deck in a miniature state.

It was getting late as the twins did their finale. Mimi changed Beezel into an eagle, and she soared up to the highest point of the mast while Hector kept a flashlight beam focused on her, for dramatic effect.

As Beezel perched atop the mast and looked out across the Amsterdam skyline, she promised herself she would come back someday and see it all again, even *Magdalena* in her new home. Then Beezel swooped down and landed on the deck in front of their small audience. They burst into applause. Mimi un-ka-poofed her and the twins took their bows.

Then, after a celebratory toast of apple cider, it was time for Hector and the girls to say goodbye.

"It's been a great adventure," Wiliken said to them. "I'm going to miss you guys. Hector, you bring these two to my next premiere, okay? I'll make sure you get the VIP treatment." Wiliken noticed the twins' long faces and said, "Hey, you two, cheer up. We'll see one another lots of times."

"How do you know?" Beezel said, trying very hard not to cry in front of him.

"I *know*, because I want to learn some magic tricks myself, and you two will have to teach me!" Then he reached inside a bag on the deck and handed Beezel and Mimi each a small wrapped box. "Here's something to remind you of our time here in Amsterdam. I found these in a box in my grandpa's house. I think he must have collected them."

"What is it?" Mimi said as she quickly tore off the wrapping paper.

Inside was a small gold box with an emerald inset on the top. "Oh, it's so pretty. Thank you, Wil."

"You're welcome. Open yours, Beezel," Wiliken said.

Beezel opened her package. She got a gold box as well, but hers had a ruby inset on the top. She was glad hers was different from Mimi's. It meant more somehow. She smiled at Wiliken. "Thank you." She was going to keep it her whole life and never, ever let it out of her sight.

"The stones are from the treasure ship," Wiliken said. "I had them added on. And guess what?

They're puzzle boxes. I want you to figure them out on your flight." He grinned at them. "Maybe it will keep you two out of trouble for ten minutes."

With that, he kissed them both on the cheek and made them promise to call him regularly. Beezel knew that in Wiliken's mind, she and Mimi really were the kid sisters he'd never had. She smiled. *Wouldn't he be surprised to find out how we feel about him?*

Uncle Hoogaboom and Wiliken were now both *very* rich men, because they had thoroughly searched the ship on the day they had unshrunk it and discovered several additional chests full of treasure.

Wiliken, although he no longer needed the money, decided that he liked acting enough to keep doing it.

Uncle Hoogaboom had other plans. With Gaidic's help, he was going to repair his damaged models and finish the model of the Noorderkerk. Then he was going to close his shop and go on a world tour.

Together, Uncle Hoogaboom and Wiliken decided that they wanted to turn Pieter Riebeeck's house into the Riebeeck Miniature Museum for children. And they wanted Gaidic to be its director.

"You still might have to zuuft a thing or two now and then for me," Uncle Hoogaboom told Hector. "Gaidic might need something for the museum."

Hector was distraught about leaving Gaidic. She had promised to come to the United States and visit him in a few short weeks, but it didn't cheer him up one bit. On the way to the airport, Beezel thought she saw actual tears in his eyes.

As the twins stood with Hector outside the airport gate on Monday morning waiting to board, Beezel thought about their visit. *Wiliken Riebeeck.* She still couldn't believe it; she and Mimi had a crush on the *same* boy. Beezel shook her head. Things certainly were going to get interesting as they got older.

Then she thought of something else. If she and Mimi moved to different places when they grew up, the magic of the Changing Coin would no longer work. Beezel cheered herself up by thinking of the fun they would have when they visited each other.

We'll make up for all that lost ka-poofing time, she told herself as she imagined Mimi and herself as two old ladies having a ka-poofing contest aboard a cruise ship.

Mimi looked positively gloomy. Beezel put her

arm around her. The steward called their row on the plane for boarding.

"It's time to go," Beezel said.

On the plane, the girls found their seats and sat down. Hector took his seat across the aisle from them.

Mimi slipped Gumdrop's plastic container out of her pocket and peeked inside it to check on Gumdrop.

While Mimi whispered to Gumdrop, Beezel stared out the window and thought about Wiliken. Her heart hurt in a scraped-knee way. *Maybe that's why they call it a crush*, she thought. She supposed it would go away in time. But then Wiliken's face floated in front of her. *Maybe not.*

She pulled her puzzle box out of her pocket and looked at it. Beezel thought about solving it and finding any hidden drawers it might have, but then she decided she wanted to save it for later. So instead, she stuffed it back down inside her pocket.

"Excuse me."

Beezel and Mimi looked up. A boy about their age, with dark eyes and curly brown hair, stood grinning down at them.

"I think you're in my seat," he said to Beezel. He

showed her his boarding pass. "But the window seat is open." He pointed to the empty seat next to her. "That must be your seat. Do you want me to take it?"

"Ah . . . uh . . ." What was the matter with her? Was this going to happen every single time a boy talked to her? *Stupid throat*, she thought as she stood up and moved over to the window seat. "That's okay, I'll move over." The boy sat down between them.

"Hi!" Mimi said cheerily. "I'm Mimi, and this is Beezel." Mimi chatted to him while Beezel stole glimpses of him from the corner of her eye.

"Barend?" she heard her sister say. "That's a nice name, isn't it, Beez?"

Beezel nodded at Barend and actually managed a smile. She looked out the window and listened to Mimi's voice as she happily told Barend about life with the Trimoni Circus. Mimi wasted no time in inviting Barend to come see them perform sometime soon.

"Right, Beezel?" Mimi said. "We can give him a backstage pass."

"Sure." Beezel nodded. This good, Mimi talking to some new boy. That was okay by her.

She hoped Mimi got a big crush on Barend. The more crushes the better. *Because that way, when we're eighteen, there's a very good chance she'll have a crush on somebody besides Wiliken.* Beezel smiled and pulled Wiliken's puzzle box out of her pocket. She fastened her seat belt and began inspecting her gift for hidden buttons or levers.

When she thought about it, she had plenty of things to look forward to.

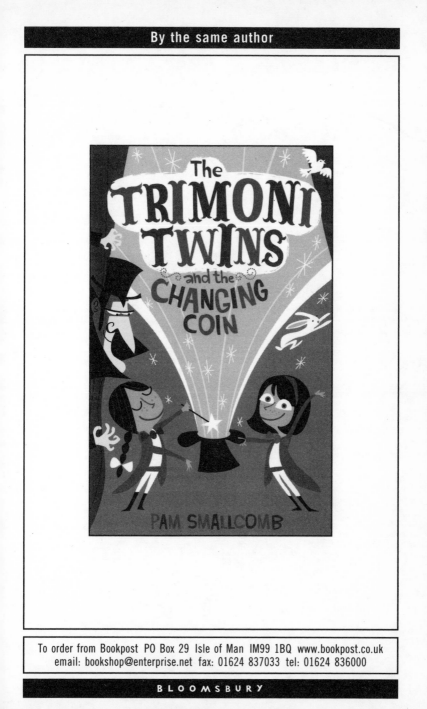